The Years Keep Rolling By

Steve Domanski

Scott Fabianek

Andrew French

CIRCLES - THE YEARS KEEP ROLLING BY

Copyright 2014 © Rabbit Valley® Books. All Rights Reserved.

Rights include the right of reproduction in whole or in part in any form, physical or electronic. Portions of this book may be reproduced for purposes of review or advertising this title for sale with written permission from Rabbit Valley.

Published and distributed through:
Rabbit Valley
5130 Fort Apache Ste 215 PMB 172
Las Vegas, NV 89148, USA.

The stories, characters, and incidents mentioned in this publication are entirely fictional. Any similarity to any person, being, or place is purely coincidental. "Rabbit Valley" is a Registered Trademark and is used with permission under license from the trademark owners.

ISBN: 978-1-62475-069-4
Printed in the United States of America.

For everyone who never stopped wanting to know the end of the story.

Published by Rabbit Valley® Books

www.rabbitvalley.com

Contents

Introduction ix

Chapter Nine: Take Your Mind Back... I Don't Know When 1

Chapter Ten, Part One: In Your Wildest Dreams 35

Chapter Ten, Part Two: Why Can't I Sing It Too? 45

Chapter Ten, Part Three: There's a Lot of Us Running Around 57

Chapter Ten, Part Four: Walking This High Road 63

Chapter Eleven: We Have to Pay for the Love We Stole 73

Chapter Twelve: Measure It in Love 107

Chapter Thirteen: Sunrise and Sundown 147

Thanks and Afterword 185

Introduction

If you're reading this without any background, you may be wondering what this weird, illustrated book is that starts with chapter nine. I feel I ought to explain.

Circles started life as a comic book that I created with my husband, Steve "iyu" Domanski, and our close friend Scott "K-9" Fabianek. We were living together in an apartment in Waltham, Ma, and we'd discussed working on a big project together. A comic called *Associated Student Bodies*, had recently ended. This 8-issue series had been the first major gay, furry comic, and no one seemed about to take it up. This was insanity to me, because so many of the people I knew in the furry fandom were gay or bi, and I was ranting about it to Steve and our friend Sean Rabbitt, who was just starting to publish comics through Rabbit Valley.

We were in the big movie house in Framingham waiting to see *Fantasia 2000*. *(The editor remembers this as being at a restaurant in Jamaica Plain near Scott's apartment like we discussed in Volume 1 of Circles. But hey, it's been a few years. –ed)* I was ranting my frustration over this situation, and Sean made the famous comment, "Why don't you do a comic together, and, if it doesn't suck, I'll publish it."

Thus challenged, Steve, Scott, and I proceeded to sit down and plan out a comic that wouldn't suck. We decided early on that the cast would be diverse, in terms of furry species, ages, body types, and so on. Influenced by my intense admiration for the musical *Rent*, I proposed that one of the characters be living with AIDS, which the others embraced. Over the next few weeks, we fleshed out six main characters and a thirteen issue storyline. We actually thought we would be able to put it out four times a year and have it come out in Real Time. We were very, very naïve in those days.

We struggled to bring the book out yearly, and the increasing demands on our time of real life, especially Scott's time, got heavier and heavier. When Scott moved out to California to try to break into animation and/or video games, the demands got even worse. After issue eight was published in 2008, I wrote issue nine, but it became slowly and increasingly clear that Scott wouldn't be able to work on any more issues.

We toyed with various ways of making it work, including contemplating doing a page every few weeks as a web-comic, but even this was clearly going to demand too much of Scott's time. For a while, I would update the news groups that wanted to know about *Circles* that we had no news to share, or that we were looking into options, and I think a lot of people thought the project was dead. Occasionally people would offer their services as an artist, but I told them that, without Scott, it wasn't *Circles*.

Well, what you hold in your hands is the final steps of this labor of love. Realizing that a comic would not be possible, I asked everyone involved how they felt about the possibility of me finishing *Circles* as a novel. Scott and Steve were enthusiastic, and Scott agreed to do some illustrations to keep a kind of visual continuity into the end.

So here it is, the ending of *Circles* that we always envisioned. I hope it was worth the wait.

Andy "Aethan" French, September 1, 2013

Special Note: The Furry Lens

We have always considered these characters humans, as viewed through a furry lens (because we like furry characters.) We've often said that you'll never hear a character complaining about getting their tail stuck in a door, or their fur being out of order, or anything of the sort. In writing the novel, I had to make a decision on whether to treat the characters as furries or humans, and I chose humans.

As a result, you may find references to things like race, body hair, and so on. Don't let it throw you. These are the same characters you've always known.

Chapter Nine: Take Your Mind Back... I Don't Know When

Dear Douglas,

    Well, winter has more or less come and gone. We're all hoping for an early spring.

    It's shocking how quiet the house can be on a day like today. With you, Jason, and Marty visiting Six Flags, Taye still on tour, Arthur and John off to the movies, and Ken at the gym, I have the house to myself. A semi-rarity these days.

    Of course, even when Ken's around, it's like he's not. I feel like something happened when he was away from us... something that's made him push even more distance between us. I keep trying to draw him out, but that just seems to make him pull back in. I think I need to just give him space. He'll tell us what he needs to when he's ready.

    It's funny... I was going to get a lot done, today. Some cleaning, some writing, maybe a spot of tea in front of the telly.

    But it turns out, I feel rather tired. I think I may just have a little nap. I'll probably feel a little better after a bit of a lie down.

Love, Paulie

Spring, 2003

Ken turned down Kinsey Circle just as the sun was beginning to get lost behind the rooftops. He sighed; he was personally done with winter, but it seemed to be clinging in wisps of chill temperature. He was ready for the days to get long and warm. Ready to put aside heavy winter coats in favor of the looser fitting clothes he preferred. Summer reminded him of the good days in Georgia, before he'd left. Before everything had gone wrong.

Things had gone wrong here, too, lately. He was still feeling ashamed about everything, about Michael, and Bo, and Paulie. Everyone he got close to seemed to turn out to be an asshole... or else he turned out to be an asshole to them. He sighed and walked to the front door, wishing he could just shove all of the crap that had been in his head lately away. It used to be easy to let go and head to a club, to let flashing lights and pounding music and hot, sweaty sex drive out anything bad. The gym used to be like that, too. When you were pushing your body, your mind could go blank. Lately, though, it wasn't the same. He was pretty sure everyone else noticed too. He felt like he was constantly sleep-walking.

He paused at the front door, getting the household's mail. He wondered why no one else had done it, but he remembered that Paulie was the only other member of the house home today. Probably, his older friend hadn't had a chance. That was cool; he liked doing little things for Paulie. God knows Paulie did enough for all of them... had always done so much for him. He fitted the key into the lock of his apartment door, heard the latch click, headed inside. Dropping his gym bag by his free weights, he sorted quickly and roughly through the mail. There was a postcard from St. Louis from Taye to everyone, and a sealed letter for Marty from him as well. There were also several letters from charities for Paulie. Not surprising. He was half-tempted to drop them all in the trash. Everyone already took so much from Paulie. But he knew that Paulie would want to see them, so he headed up the stairs to the loft apartment that Paulie and Doug shared.

"Hey, Paulie?" he called. "I brought in the mail." No answer, but it was possible Paulie was at the far end of the loft and wouldn't have heard. He made his way up and paused. Everything seemed oddly still. "Paulie?"

He came around the doorframe and stopped. Paulie was there, crumpled and lying on the floor beside his writing desk. The journal he was writing in was still open on the desk. A few bounding steps and Ken was down on his knees next to Paulie, fearing the worst. To his relief, Paulie gave a soft groan. "Oh, my God, Paulie... c'mon! Wake up, man!" He shook him a little, getting another soft groan. He wanted to lift Paulie up, to put him in bed... but he thought he remembered something about not moving people who've fallen, in case they've hurt their backs or necks. Did that apply here?

"Ken?" Paulie groaned weakly. "Oh, dear, I'm so sorry... I must've... fainted. I was feeling very light-headed."

Ken heaved a sigh of relief as Paulie managed to sit up a little. Ken put his arm around the older man's back and shoulders, helping him sit up. "Let's just get you onto the couch, buddy. And then I'll call Dr. Roberts."

• • • • • • • • • • • • •

Ken sat on the edge of Paulie's bed, watching Dr. Roberts examine Paulie thoroughly. Pulse, blood pressure, a look into the eyes and ears. Finally, the doctor sighed. "Well, as far as I can tell, you just stood up, got dizzy, and passed out. Do you remember how you felt?"

Paulie looked chagrinned. "Normal aches and pains, but those've been around for ages. Mostly light-headed. Dizzy, yes. What a silly thing to have happen. A fainting spell. Like I'm the heroine of some bloody Victorian romance. I'm such a ninny at times."

The doctor chuckled, stroking the tufted beard at the end of his chin. "What you are is lucky. Lucky that you didn't bang your head on anything on the way down, and that someone found you so fast."

Paulie smiled a little at Ken, who lowered his eyes, feeling self-conscious. "Well, I'm lucky, doctor," Paulie said softly. "I have plenty of family around to keep an eye on me."

The doctor raised an eyebrow. "Why do you think I've supported your decision to stay at home rather than look into clinical care? You have more people looking after you here than a team of nurses."

Paulie chuckled, and then frowned. "Is this going to keep happening? Dizzy spells? Passing out?"

Dr. Roberts sighed, softly. "Paulie, I'm going to be candid, because I know you prefer it that way. You have to remember that HIV doesn't come with a check-list or a manual. Symptoms come and go. Some people live years healthily, and others deteriorate quickly. You've been more lucky than most. You have to accept that you're not going to stay healthy forever." He paused as Paulie exhaled a held breath. Then he patted his old friend's shoulder. "Now, I've taken a sample of your blood, and I'll run some tests, but I might need you to come in to the office. You're sure you won't consider coming in so I can run more tests? I can arrange for you to have a private room."

Paulie frowned a little. "Gene, you know how I feel about hospitals..."

Dr. Roberts chuckled. "Well, of course. It's not like I do housecalls for all of my patients. You're pretty much the only one." He took off his glasses, rubbed his eyes, then looked at Paulie seriously. "Just promise me that when I tell you that you *need* to come to the clinic, you will?"

Paulie leaned back in the pillows, looking more relaxed. "You know I will. Thank you, Gene, for everything. Truly."

Dr. Roberts smiled, warmly. "You're welcome. And I'll be back tomorrow to check on you. Please get some rest tonight. No night owling."

Paulie closed his eyes, still smiling. "Hoot hoot."

Ken stood up. "I'll see you to the door. Dr. Roberts."

The doctor shook his head. "I know the way, Ken, thank you. And you can call me Gene. I think you've been coming to see me long enough to have earned it. Especially if you're going to be helping this one out." He jerked his head at Paulie, indicating who he meant, and Ken smiled and nodded.

"Thanks, Gene," said Ken. "I really appreciate you seeing him on such short notice."

The doctor coughed a little, uncomfortably. "Yes, well, I owe Paulie more than I can conveniently repay. He's donated enough money to the free clinic that we should probably build a new expansion and name it after him." Dr. Roberts looked at Paulie, then back at Ken. "See that he takes it easy, alright, Ken?"

Ken smiled. "I will, Gene. Thanks again, and have a good night."

As Dr. Roberts headed down the stairs, Ken stood there, listening to Paulie breathing, behind him. Finally he said. "So... I called Doug. They're on their way back."

Ken heard Paulie sigh. "Oh dear. I really didn't want to spoil their day at the parks."

Ken shrugged, half-turning, mind churning. "He said they were already walking to the car when I called. It'll still be an hour or more til they get back, but the movie'll be over soon, so Arthur and John will be back."

Paulie smiled, softly, at his young friend. Of all of the Kinsey Street Inhabitants, Ken held a special place in his heart. Maybe because, inside, Paulie felt Ken really needed him. How ironic to have the tables turned, to need Ken so much. "You don't have to nursemaid me, if you have plans," he said with a chuckle. "It was just a dizzy spell."

Ken chuckled, weakly. "I don't know how you stay so strong. When the doctor called and told me I was negative, I feel like I had a nervous breakdown. I don't know how you manage to be so cool."

Paulie thought about it. "I don't know if I'm strong, dear. There just isn't much I can do about it, so I try to be positive. To take life as it comes. To enjoy every day I have."

Ken slowly turned to look at Paulie. He looked thin, Ken thought, pale. Ken felt a tremble start somewhere inside him, some part fear, some part anger. "It's just... you don't..." He clenched his hands into fists as his emotions boiled over and spilled out into an expression of pain. "Paulie, you can't... I can't lose you!"

Paulie's shock was palpable. This wasn't what he expected at all from the younger man. "Lose me?" he asked. "Ken, what... what're you...?" He stopped as Ken came closer, sitting on the edge of the bed. Paulie resisted an urge to put a calming hand on Ken's knee; he didn't know exactly what Ken was thinking, and he didn't want the defensive walls to pop back up.

Finally, Ken half-turned, looking at him. Paulie could read so many things on the young man's face — grief, rage, shame... When he spoke, his voice was calm, but it broke slightly, betraying the storm inside the words. "I just..." He hesitated, then pushed forward. "I could really tell you anything, right? And you'll listen? And you won't be angry, or hate me?"

Paulie's heart ached, and he finally did touch Ken's arm, gently, and the younger man flinched away and rubbed when Paulie had touched him. Paulie ventured, "Ken, you know I care for you a great deal. If you want to talk about what happened with you and Bo…"

Ken shook his head with a sigh. "That's just it. You already know everything that happened with Bo. But when I was there, I remembered some… things. About when I was a kid."

Paulie blinked. "Oh." Ken had always been evasive about his youth in Georgia, insisting there wasn't much to tell. "You've never really wanted to talk much about that, dear."

Ken was quiet for a few moments, looking down at his hands. "Well… it's weird. I almost feel like I didn't remember it all until recently. Like I kind of walled it off, you know? And when Bo and I fought… it's like it broke through the wall." He chuckled, bitterly. "Maybe I should be grateful to him."

Paulie pushed some pillows behind him to sit up a bit more. "Ken, you can talk to me about anything you need to. I'm always here for you."

Ken looked at his friend's face. Paulie had always been so decent. So non-judgmental. If anyone in the world could hear the story and still love him, it would be Paulie. "Okay, then," he sighed, feeling the great relief of just beginning the story.

• • • • • • • • • • • • •

Well, let's see. I was born in Georgia, you know that. My family's lived there for generations, but Grammaw said we could trace our lines clear across the ocean… heck, we still have family back in South Africa. I guess there's no secret how my family ended up in Georgia, but that's not really part of my story, directly.

We weren't exactly poor, but we sure as heck weren't well off. Lower middle class, I guess you'd say. Or upper lower? Who knows how to define those things?

If you want to imagine the house I lived in, think of a one-story affair with a little porch and a decent sized shed out back. It was in relatively good condition, with white paint and a bit of green trim. And if the white had gotten a little dingy over the years, and the green was peeling, I didn't much care as a kid, any more than I cared that the car we had was ten years or more too late to be called new, or that the food we ate was chicken more often than beef. It was my home, and I loved every scrap of it. From the tire swing on the old willow tree in the front yard to every dandelion-covered inch of the back yard. It was my domain.

We lived in Lexington, Georgia. It wasn't a big town, and it was in about as good a shape as our house and car was. Every once in a great while, when we'd go into town and see a movie or eat in a restaurant there, it was a big deal.

I was a really scrawny kid, gap-toothed, knobby knees with scabs on 'em. Always running everywhere I went. My Mama always said I was born early out of being so restless and that I'd never slowed down.

I almost always ran around with my old neighborhood gang. Other black kids, like me. There was Cale, who was kind of fat, but all smiles. He was like our group comedian. There was Jerome, who stuttered a little. We used to tease him a bit and call him Ja-Ja-Jerome, but he was our buddy. And there was Tina. Tina was my best friend, in a lot of ways. She was big… kind of like Gus, really. Maybe that's why I took to Gus so much when we met.

I remember the three of them so well. I felt like they were all I had, at times. Funny that I've remembered them so well and forgotten so much of everything else.

They weren't *all* I had, of course. I had Mama, an' Grammaw. Grammaw was my Mama's mama, and she lived in the same neighborhood. She came to dinner most every night. Daddy had left when I was four, so I hardly remember him. I kind of missed having a Daddy, but I got by. I don't know why he left, because Mama was beautiful, and I don't mean that in the sense that every kid thinks his Mama is beautiful. She was a really pretty lady, and everyone used to tell her she should be an actress or a model. She'd always smile and say she was happy being just who she was. She worked in a factory outside of town, making shoes, I think it was. I know I always had new shoes, even when nothing else was new.

Grammaw was wonderful, and she made up for a lot of what we didn't have. She was like an angel, sometimes. I remember, she'd give me a cookie to eat as she was peeling apples for a pie, and she'd tell me her stories. Stories about people she knew, or that she'd known, and all the funny things they'd done. And we'd just sit there together, laughing.

She never told stories about Uncle Davis, though, so I was kind of surprised when he showed up at the door one day when I was ten. He'd been in the army, and the government bus had dropped him off down the road. When Mama saw him coming down the driveway, she squealed and ran off the porch to hug him. I'd never seen her so happy. Davis was her little brother, and they'd been really close as kids.

I remember looking him over. He was probably about Marty's age, rangy and lean and all hard muscles from the military training. He was wearing his army fatigues, and he had a big olive-green rucksack over his back. When Mama introduced me, I was kind of shy, but he took a baseball out of his pack and offered it to me. I remember Grammaw put her hand on my shoulder and steered me over to him, but she kept her hand there as I took the ball from him, and it tightened a little bit when he patted my head.

I thought Uncle Davis was exciting and fun. He seemed to like me right away, and I liked him, too. I couldn't understand why Grammaw didn't seem happy. He was her son; you'd think she'd be glad he was back. But she always seemed to be watching him, when she was around, and not with a smile. One evening, while we were setting on the porch, and Grammaw was sewing, I asked her about it. She said that Uncle Davis had been "troubled" when he was younger. He'd gone into the army to try and get his act together. She hoped he had.

That summer he came home… that's one of the best times I can remember. I hung out with Uncle Davis almost as much as I did with my Old Gang. Sometimes we'd all hang out together. Uncle Davis found his old baseball glove from when he was a kid and gave it to me. We played a lot of catch together, and we'd talk about stuff. One day, after he'd gone to meet some old army buddies, he brought me home an official Atlanta Braves baseball cap. It was way too big for me, but I wore it all that summer anyway.

Sometimes, when it was too hot to play, the Old Gang, and Mama, and Uncle Davis, and I all sat on the porch. Mama made lemonade, and we'd sit and listen to some of Uncle Davis' stories. He told us he'd been in Grenada, which none of us exactly understood, but he told awesome and scary war stories. Sometimes Mama would have to tell him to tone it down, because he'd get a little overexcited in his descriptions and give us nightmares. He had a cool knife that he said he'd taken from a "Commie" in Grenada.

Things were going really well for Uncle Davis. He got a job at a local auto shop, and he had an apartment in town, so he could visit often. Even Grammaw seemed to get over her concerns about how Davis had been "troubled." Everyone was happy, especially me. Some of my fondest memories were of curling up on the couch between Uncle Davis and Mama in my pajamas, and all of us watching TV together. I finally understood what having a Daddy meant. Uncle Davis was like that for me.

But then things got bad.

I remember, I was on the porch with Mama, and she was pouring lemonade. Uncle Davis' car stopped in the driveway, and he got out. I jumped off the porch and ran to hug him, because he always hugged me when he came over. But this time, he just walked on by me, like he hadn't seen me there. He had a six-pack dangling from his hand, with a couple already missing, and he seemed angry.

He'd lost his job at the auto shop. The owner had said that it wasn't him in particular. Times were just tight. But Uncle Davis took it real bad. The next few times I saw him, he always had that six-pack in his hands. He drank a lot, and he stopped paying so much attention to me and coming over so often.

Uncle Davis and Grammaw started fighting a lot. Grammaw said that the army hadn't changed him one bit. He was still the same as ever. Uncle Davis didn't like that one bit. One night, at the dinner table, they yelled so much, and I covered my ears and clenched my eyes shut real tight, just wanting it to be quiet. Grammaw told Uncle Davis to leave, and I was afraid he'd go away forever.

Mama didn't let that happen, though. She thought Grammaw was overreacting. She told Davis that, if he needed to, he could fix up the old shed out back of the house and stay there as long as he needed to. He could just pay some money when he could afford it and help out with groceries. Grammaw didn't like that at all, but she didn't say anything.

Naturally, I helped fix the place up. I loved the idea of Uncle Davis sleeping right out back. He wired it up with lights… he was really handy when he wasn't drinking. We moved out the old junk and carried the trundle bed out from the house. Uncle Davis said that he was happy to bivouac back there, and that it was comfier than Uncle Sam's cots.

One box we found had a bunch of old dirty magazines in them. I don't know if they were Dad's, or what. I was the one opened the box, and my jaw dropped, seeing a woman's titties right there on display. Uncle Davis laughed and pulled one out, looking through it. He said we'd save that box, as he'd enjoy looking through them.

I thought Uncle Davis wouldn't want me to see those magazines, but he didn't seem to mind. He told me stories about girls he'd been with in Grenada, and other places he'd traveled. He said some of them hadn't been much older than me. Talking about it made me feel weird, but I liked that Uncle Davis and I had this secret, too. I never told Mama or Grammaw. Uncle Davis said I could come out to the shed any time he was there and look at the magazines but not to do it when he wasn't around, in case Mama caught me.

Uncle Davis took various odd-jobs around the neighborhood for a little cash here and there. He never really did give Mama much money for rent or groceries, but he always seemed to have a few dollars for beer. Grammaw didn't really come around for supper any more, although I was welcome at her house any time. I don't think she wanted to be around Uncle Davis.

The next summer eventually came, and Uncle Davis still didn't have a new job. He let his military crew-cut go longer, and he got a little paunchy. Around that time, Tina's Mom stopped letting her come over to play. I didn't know why at the time, and Tina wouldn't talk about it, but some kids said that it was because of Uncle Davis... that Tina's Mom didn't like Uncle Davis for some reason. Maybe from before he left for the army. It was sad, but with just the guys, we could play football and some games Tina wouldn't play.

Mama started working a second job, because the money from the shoe factory wasn't stretching far enough. She got a job waiting tables at a diner in town, and sometimes I could go with Uncle Davis and have dinner there. It made me sad; she always seemed tired. I sometimes wondered why she didn't push Uncle Davis to find a job, and I started trying to find little things I could do to help out. I mowed some lawns, got a paper route... that kind of thing.

One night, Mama called and talked to Uncle Davis. He said that she was pulling a second shift at the diner, because one of the others was home sick. She wouldn't be home until real late, and Uncle Davis and I would have to look out for ourselves. Uncle Davis was cool. He took out some money he'd stashed and bought us some fried chicken, and we talked and ate and we were having a good time.

Afterwards, I got my pajamas on, and we sprawled and watched TV together, like we used to. Uncle Davis was drinking a beer, and he seemed kind of restless and thoughtful. When he got another beer, he offered to let me have one. I knew Mama would never have let him do that when she was around. It made me feel kind of grown-up and sneaky.

I thought it tasted awful, of course, and Uncle Davis chuckled at that, but he told me to drink it up, because he didn't want to waste it. I didn't want to disappoint him, so I did it of course, and he put his arm around my shoulders, telling me what a big boy I was now. I felt weird after drinking the beer… kind of spacey and good… but also afraid Mama would know I'd done it, and I'd get punished. Uncle Davis promised she wouldn't know, but then he kind of cozied me in close to him, and he told me I was a pretty boy.

I didn't know what to think of that. Girls are pretty, but boys are handsome, and told him that. He laughed and said that I was as pretty as a little girl. I didn't think much of that as a compliment, and I started feeling really odd.

And then he touched me.

• • • • • • • • • • • • •

Ken looked at Paulie, his face more set and determined than anything. "Uncle Davis just reached over with the hand that wasn't around my shoulders, and he touched me. He… he didn't stop. He pushed his hand inside my pajamas, and…." He trailed off, his expression unreadable for a moment.

Paulie didn't say anything, but he knew that his expression had to be shocked. Ken looked at him and shrank a bit under it. "Do you… think I'm a bad person for letting that happen?"

Paulie was even more taken aback, his horror at what Ken had said about his uncle overwhelmed by this new feeling. "You? Oh… oh, Ken. Dear boy. No, of course not. It's not your fault. You were only eleven. Your Uncle was taking a terrible advantage of you. You must know that."

Ken looked down at his knees. "Yeah, I guess I know. But that's not what I thought at the time. I thought I must be… bad. Wrong. I thought I must've done something… said something to make him think I wanted this." He ran his hand through his short hair. "And, you know… I did want it, on some levels. It was attention from him. I loved having him pay attention to me again, even like that. I'd hated it when he didn't have time for me any more."

Ken had a haunted look, and Paulie yearned again to touch him, but he didn't dare. He'd never seen the young man look so vulnerable in the time they'd known each other. Ken had been so distant since he'd come home from Bo's the previous winter. Paulie was afraid that touching him would pop everything like a soap bubble. He waited, and, eventually, Ken began again.

• • • • • • • • • • • • •

Uncle Davis started finding lots of time for me after that. But it was to do those things he wanted. Things that made me feel so bad. I would sneak out to the shed after Mama was asleep, and we would… be together.

Mama probably noticed my mood changing, but, between the fact that she was working two jobs and that I was slipping into puberty, I suspect she thought I was just going through hormonal changes. Uncle Davis warned me not to tell her anything, because then everyone would find out that I was a faggot, and then none of my friends would ever talk to me again. I believed him, too. My Old Gang used words like faggot and homo as some of the worst insults we could. I figured that, if they knew I really was one, I'd be all alone for good. And thanks to Uncle Davis, I absolutely believed that's what I was, so I did what he wanted for years, and I didn't tell anyone.

By the time I turned thirteen, I was going out to the shed a few times a week. Puberty was raging in full force, and I was growing up fast. My thirteenth birthday started out really nice. There was a big dinner, with all my favorite things, and a chocolate cake with buttercream icing my Mama had gotten at the diner, and she delayed going in, to spend time with me. After she left, though, Uncle Davis told me to come out to the shed. That he had a special surprise waiting for me.

I went out, and it felt… different. We drank beers together, and he actually seemed nice, and happy. He had a real present for me — a new baseball cap to replace the one I'd now outgrown. But he also said that I was getting really grown-up, so he had something new to teach me. He'd been looking forward to it.

He got kind of nervous, and we both got pretty drunk. After a while, he had me lay down on my belly, and he got on top… and he told me it would hurt some, but not for long…

• • • • • • • • • • • •

Ken choked out a sob, as it all seemed to come back to him, and he hugged his arms around his slender body, reflexively.

Paulie knew that he was crying too, the tears unable to be held back as he saw all the shame and pain his friend had endured. He swiped at his eyes and murmured, "Oh my God. Oh, Ken, I'm so sorry."

Ken stammered, tears openly rolling down his cheeks. "I… I just…" He looked over at Paulie, the conflict on his face like a knife in the older man's gut. "You've got to understand, Paulie, I loved him, even with everything he'd done. I loved him so much. He was like a Daddy to me. He told me that this is what faggots did together, to show that they loved each other."

Ken buried his face in his hands, his anguish palpable. "I didn't understand why God was letting this happen to me. I knew from church that God hated faggots. Did he hate them so much that he made them hurt each other for love? I was so disgusted and confused." Ken balled his fists and pushed them against the side of his head. "I wanted to kill Uncle Davis for what he was doing. But… I also couldn't stop going out to the shed to be with him. I thought that God must hate me for being a faggot. That's why he was letting him hurt me so much."

Paulie was quiet, letting Ken cry, letting him get the pain out. Eventually, Ken quieted and continued in a voice that was raw now from emotion.

• • • • • • • • • • • •

I was angry all the time, but everyone thought I was just a really difficult teenager. Deep inside, I hated everyone for letting these things happen to me. I hated the Old Gang for using the word faggot so much, reminding me of who I was. I especially hated Tina. Every time she saw me, she had this pitying, concerned look on her face. I don't know how, but I was sure she knew what was happening to me. I hated her for knowing my awful secret.

It didn't help that I really was gay. I would get these feelings around guys. Like showering after gym class, my body would react, and I couldn't help it. I got into fights, and I was growing, but I was still scrawny and skinny, so I got beat up a lot. Even the Old Gang started giving me a wide berth. I caught them whispering about me, or looking at me and getting quiet as I got closer. I hated them all for not helping me. I stopped hanging out with them.

I was especially angry with Mama. Her work had her away more and more often, so he had more and more time alone with me. I hated her so much for not knowing what he was doing to me. Or knowing and not caring. I was so messed up, I didn't know which it was.

I know this is going to sound funny, but, all jokes aside, thank God for the local YMCA. I scraped together enough money to register in an after school program there, and I got to swim, and learn some boxing, and run track, and tons of stuff. When I was working my body, I learned to let my mind go kind of blank and stop thinking about everything. It was a good place to get away from what was happening at home.

The only problem was that, eventually, I always had to go home.

See, no one talked about kids getting abused like that in those days. Not in my town, at least. That was something that happened in the big cities, or up North, so no one was aware of it. Nowadays, there'd be warning signs, concerned parent groups, the Internet to find out how to get help. But not then. Then I felt isolated. Alone. Out of control. I didn't know what to do, or who to tell. Plus Uncle Davis had started warning me about what *he* would do if I did tell anyone.

I thought I was trapped. I even thought about killing myself a few times. But then something happened, and help came from a direction I didn't expect. I was at a local field, on the way to the Y. I remember, there were some kids playing baseball, and I was feeling miserable, when someone walked up behind me. I thought it might be Uncle Davis at first, but it was Tina. I almost walked away, but she stopped me. Something about her expression, this time. She was sad, and ashamed, and she asked me point blank if Uncle Davis was doing something to me.

I was shocked, and I felt that wave of hate for her knowing again, but then she told me what I probably should've guessed, if I hadn't been so wrapped up in what was happening to me. Uncle Davis had touched her, too. He hadn't done everything to her that he had with me, thank God, but he'd done some. That's why her Mom didn't let her come to our house any more. They hadn't gone to the police, because they didn't want my family to go through the shame, but they hadn't imagined he would turn his attentions on a boy instead. On me.

I did start walking away, then, feeling sick in my stomach. But she followed me. I told her to leave me alone. That I was a faggot and she should just leave me alone. She told me she didn't care if I was a faggot. She was my friend, and I didn't deserve to be hurt. She wanted to help me. She even said that she didn't think God hated faggots after all, because why would he make them like that and then hate them. No one had ever talked to me like that before.

I stopped. We walked someplace quiet and sat and talked, and I told her everything that was happening. I didn't want her pitying me. But, oh my God, it felt so good to be able to talk to someone. Not to feel so alone any more. I remember hugging her so hard, crying so much. I never loved any other girl like I loved her.

After that talk, I wasn't such a willing partner for Uncle Davis any more, but he didn't much care now if I wanted it or not. He was still a lot bigger than I was, and he wanted what he wanted. If I tried to fight him, he'd beat me up and do what he wanted anyway. So I did what he wanted… for a while, anyway.

See, I was getting bigger. I was going to the Y all the time, pounding the punching bags, getting ready, because I didn't intend to be Uncle Davis' faggot for the rest of my life. By the time I was seventeen, I was almost as tall as he was, and I was in way better shape than he was. I swore to myself that this was coming to an end, one way or another.

One night, I was ready. I went to the shed and found Uncle Davis there, rip-roaring drunk. There were empty beer cans and whiskey bottles all over the floor, and he gave me this smile that made my stomach turn over. I told Davis that I'd kill him before I let him touch me again. He didn't like that one bit, and he let his punches and kicks do the talking. I might've been in better shape, but Uncle Davis did have army training, and he was still pretty goddamned fast. I got in a few licks, but he finally kicked me in the stomach, and I fell to the ground, feeling like I was going to vomit blood.

But, when I hit the floor, I saw what could set me free. His commie knife was under the trundle bed. I rolled to the side and grabbed it, even as he was hauling me up, maybe to throw me onto the bed, I don't know. I slashed out, and I caught him along his left cheek. I saw the blood spurt out, and he screamed, fell back on the floor, on his ass, scattering empty beer cans and bottles when he hit. He put his hand up to his cheek, and the blood kept running between his fingers. "Hell's wrong wit'chu, boy?" he asked. I think, in his mind, what we were doing was still something I must want, because I kept coming to the shed. He actually looked surprised at what had happened.

I… I don't know what I felt. I was terrified. I think I actually thought to myself that I could go to prison for knifing a veteran. Can you believe that? The dumb shit we think of. I must've dropped the knife and run, because the next thing I remember clearly, I was at Tina's house. She had this big sycamore tree right outside her bedroom, and I climbed up it and threw pennies at her window until she opened it.

I told her I was leaving, even though I didn't have a dollar to my name and only the clothes off of my back. I was leaving, and I wasn't coming back. She looked at me with a sad sort of expression. I think that she was kind of sweet on me, even knowing what I was. She had this big Mason jar that was jammed with money. She'd been saving her money to go to Europe after high school. But she gave it to me, pretty much forced me to take it. She told me I could pay her back once I was on my feet. She leaned way out of her window to give it to me, and I leaned in. And she kissed me. Only time I ever kissed a girl.

At the bus station, I counted out the money, and I bought a ticket for as far away as I could get. That turned out to be Boston, and I lived on the streets for a few weeks, until I found a bar that only seemed to have guys in it. I found that I looked old enough to pass for drinking age. I also found that there were guys who would buy you beer, or food, or clothes, or anything else, if you were a pretty boy who'd flatter them and do what they wanted.

Joe was great for that. He had money to burn, and having a hot young guy on his arm made everyone else jealous. He moved me into his house, and I got to live in the lap of luxury for a while. That's when I met John, and through him, you, and Doug, and Arthur, and Taye, and everyone.

I think that, if I'd let it happen, Joe would've kept taking care of me. Part of me, however, decided that I had a new motto: Do unto others, before they do unto you. I started seeing other guys for just long enough to get what I wanted from them, and then going on to other guys. As long as I kept everyone at a distance, no one could hurt me again.

• • • • • • • • • • • •

Ken looked over at Paulie, a slightly rueful smile on his face. "Joe was pretty pissed off when he found I'd been with other guys, too. I think he felt humiliated. He tossed me out, and I had nowhere to go. I was shocked when you came over and talked to me in the park and told me I could stay at your place, because I didn't understand why."

Ken looked down at the floor. "You didn't want anything from me, Paulie. You just cared about me, from when we'd talked before. I think you saw something decent in me that I hadn't seen for a long time."

Ken was quiet for a while, then shrugged. "You know the rest. I got modeling jobs. I've had boyfriends and playmates, and I haven't really let anyone in." He looks at his hands. "I might've let Michael in, eventually. I think I was this close to letting him in... really letting him in. And that scared me. So I went out alone one night, and that's when I met Bo, and..." He gestured, helplessly, and stopped talking.

Paulie swiped his hand over his eyes and then replaced his glasses. "And... you've just remembered, all of this? What do they call it? Recovered memories?"

Ken shrugged. "I didn't forget it, exactly. It's more like I just refused to ever think about it. Like I said before, I walled it off. I never wanted to talk about it or think about it again." He looked at Paulie, looked into those warm, brown eyes. "When Bo came along, I think there was something kind of like Uncle Davis about him." He dropped his gaze again. "I felt that same kind of helplessness. Like everything was out of my control."

Ken held up his hands, looked at them as he turned them over. "When we fought, it just... it all came flooding back. I felt like I was suffocating. I had to get out of there."

The two men sat silently, neither one sure what to say to the other. Paulie couldn't find the comforting words adequate to the task. Ken knew there was something unresolved between them, knew what he had to say, but it scared him. Finally, however, without looking at Paulie, he said, "There was one other person who got close. You got close."

Paulie looked up. "Eh? Close? Me?"

Ken turned, half-smiling. "I couldn't help but let you get close to me. You just slipped inside my defenses when I wasn't ready. Part of me was always waiting for you to hurt me." Tears welled up, started flowing down his cheeks. "But you never hurt me. I'm the one who hurt you."

Paulie felt an ache for his friend's pain. "Oh, Ken…" he began, but the younger man stopped him.

"No, I gotta say this. See, when I left, I said you weren't my Dad." He reached out, took Paulie's hands in his. "It was a lie. I love you, Paulie. You've been the best father a guy… any guy… could ever have."

Paulie was crying too, now, and the two reached out for each other, hugged each other, held each other closely. He could hear the smile in Ken's voice from near his ear, although the tears were still flowing. "I love you so much, Paulie."

Paulie sighed, then quietly returned, "I love you too, dear."

They were quiet for a long while, holding each other. Ken felt so much tension leaving him in the flood of his tears. Finally, he pushed back a bit, laughed as he swiped at his eyes. "Some nursemaid I am, huh? You need the TLC, and I end up sobbing in your arms."

Paulie smiled, patted Ken's hand. All the tension from Ken's leaving felt dispersed between them. Paulie thought that Ken seemed closer than he had in years to the vulnerable Georgia boy he'd first been when they'd met. After a moment, he thought of something, hesitated, and then asked, "I don't want to bring up anything else that might be painful, but… do you know what happened to your Uncle?"

Ken nodded, looking a little grim. "Yeah. I've kept in touch with Tina. After I left, she went to my Mama and told her everything. Mama called the cops, and he was arrested. They couldn't get him on anything to do with me, since I wasn't around to testify, but Tina testified about the things he did to her and he got sent to prison." He sighed. "She was always braver than I was."

Ken looked down again, but Paulie thought that a fierce sort of gladness was in his eyes. "I hear he got killed in prison. Even murderers don't take kindly to guys who do… what he did."

Paulie nodded, a little relieved that Ken must've gotten some resolution from that news, no matter how grim it was. "What about the rest of your family?"

Ken looked away. "My Mama's still alive. Grammaw died a couple of years after I left. I thought about going back for the funeral, but..." He paused, thinking, and then said, "There was too much unresolved. Too much I didn't want to have to explain to people." He looked back at Paulie's face. "I still talk to Tina sometimes... e-mail, or phone. I've sent my Mama a few birthday and Christmas cards so she knows I'm alright. But I don't include my forwarding address, and my information here is unpublished, so I don't think she knows where I am." He looked a bit miserable. "I've never had the nerve to call."

Ken sighed, feeling exhausted, worn out from having opened up so completely. "I don't know what to do now. I had to fix things with you, but I feel like I wrecked everything else good in my life when I moved over to Bo's."

Paulie smiled a little. "Well, you know how you fix that, dear?" Ken looked over, and Paulie patted his cheek. "One thing at a time."

● ● ● ● ● ● ● ● ● ● ● ● ●

Michael Lang was out with a few buddies at the Fritz Lounge, and they'd had a few after-work beers and commiserated on crappy ex-boyfriends. He hadn't talked about Ken, partly because he didn't want to find out that any of the rest of them had a "Ken" story. Could he even claim ex-boyfriend status? Ken didn't normally use the b-word. Ken was more of an ex-whatever. Mike hadn't started dating again. He hadn't really wanted to. He told himself he wasn't moping, but he wasn't sure if he believed himself.

As they came out and said their goodbyes, heading for the subway, he was shocked to see Ken leaning against the wall. He'd heard that Ken had come home, but there'd been no sign of him at any clubs. At first, he felt relief at seeing him, but that quickly gave way to anger. Here was the guy who'd made it quite clear that there was no point in them seeing each other again. Was his being here a coincidence? He'd mentioned where he was going to John. Was it possible the bookstore owner had arranged this? If so, there were going to be some angry words.

As Mike and the others got closer, Ken saw them. He straightened up, smiled at Michael, and then noticed the other's scowl. "Hey," he said, voice careful neutral.

Mike didn't try to hide his irritation. "Oh. Hey," he said.

Ken looked the group over. The others were looking back and forth between the two. "Um… you got a minute?"

Mike's friend Tony arched an eyebrow. "Mike? You cool?"

Mike nodded, folding his arms. "Yeah. You guys go ahead. I'll be fine."

Ken waited til the others were gone, hands shoved into the pockets of the light spring jacket he was wearing. "So… I was a complete asshat, pretty much."

Was this an apology? Mike didn't want one. He kept his voice neutral, to the best of his ability. "Yeah, no argument here."

Ken nodded, looked painfully awkward. Mike almost felt sorry for him. Almost. Ken continued, "I'm not asking you to forgive me without knowing more about what happened…"

Mike shrugged, trying to be nonchalant, and launched into what he'd planned to say if they ever spoke again. "Ken, save it. I've talked to a lot of your ex-boyfriends before. Heck, I was roommates with one of them, remember? No, you probably don't. Anyway, I get it. You come in, you have some fun, and you go. That's your thing. I get it." Mike didn't pause… didn't want to let Ken interrupt him. "I thought we had something more. Silly me. I got burned. My fault."

"But that's just it," Ken blurted out, spreading his hands. "You weren't wrong, and it wasn't your fault! That's what I wanted to tell you…"

Mike held up a hand to forestall Ken. He didn't want to hear this. "Ken, I have to go. I got over it, okay? Whatever." Ken's face was falling, and Michael almost melted, but he pushed on. "I don't have the energy to hang out with you and make you feel better about yourself and make you feel okay about what you did right now. I'm going home to have dinner."

As he started to walk away, Mike felt an ache inside. He knew Ken was watching him as he walked by, but he couldn't bring himself to look at that sad face, that expression of misery. Just as he got to the street-crossing, he heard Ken blurt out, "Wait!"

"What?" Mike grumbled, feeling real annoyance twinge up his spine. He felt betrayed by the streetlight that was insistently telling him not to walk when he really wanted to get away.

"I don't want you to make me feel better about myself," Ken said, coming up beside him. "I just want to hang out."

Mike rolled his eyes. "Ken, look…"

Ken was the one to hold up his hands, this time. Almost in a gesture of truce. "Not sex. Just to talk."

Mike blinked at that. "You… want to talk?"

"Yes," Ken said, nodding his head for emphasis. "If you're hungry, Emilio's is right around the corner. They have awesome pizza and really good egg salad. I just wanna talk, okay?"

Mike was sure his expression was a little incredulous, or at least skeptical. "But… you don't talk, remember?"

Ken groaned. "Yeah, it sucked that I said that. Look, at the very least, you deserve to hear some stuff. It might help you understand why I was such a douchebag. I'm not going to make some heartfelt plea and say, 'Oh, come back. Things'll be different.' You don't deserve that shit." Then he sighed. "But I'd *like* them to be different. Okay? This is all new to me." Then he gave an endearingly sheepish grin. "I'm not used to being on this end of things."

There was a pause. Both men regarded each other. Mike had to admit that he'd never seen Ken look more open or honest. He regarded his ex-whatever with uncertainty… but maybe a little hope, too.

"Emilio's?" he asked. "Right around the corner? Their egg salad is awesome?"

Ken nodded. "Pretty much the best. Pickle relish. Bit of mustard."

Mike sighed. "Well… okay. Just to talk. And eat."

Ken nodded, a hint of smile playing on his lips. "Best behavior, I promise."

The two walked down the street. They weren't arm in arm, or even particularly close, but there was a feeling around them. A feeling of hope. That maybe, what they'd had was something more, and that it still had a chance. Maybe.

● ● ● ● ● ● ● ● ● ● ● ●

Ken returned to his apartment feeling bolder. The talk with Michael had gone better than he had probably deserved. He thought there might still be something there, and he looked forward to finding out on the future.

For now, though, there was one other wrong desperately in need of righting, and one that he couldn't put off any longer.

He picked up the phone, dialed a number he hadn't called in nearly a decade but still knew by heart. The phone rang, and he wondered if he really wanted there to be anyone home or not. After a few rings, however, there was a click and someone picked up on the other end. He knew the voice at once, of course, and he felt a thick wave of emotion hit. "H-hello?" he said, feeling like a little boy again. The person at the other end asked who was calling, and he almost faltered, but he had come too far to stop now. In a voice he hardly recognized as his own, he said, softly, "Hello, Mama. It's me. Ken."

Dear Douglas,

Spring is finally here! How lovely!

Ken's much more himself these days. Not all that long ago, I worried that Ken would always be alone. Now, seeing that Michael and Ken have been seeing more of each other... I'm not so sure.

Ken promises everything with Michael is just friendly, for now. He's leaving the next step up to Michael.

Seeing Michael look at Ken, though... I think Ken told him everything, too. I think there's forgiveness there. And real affection.

Seeing how Michael looks at Ken, I doubt they'll stay just friends for long.

Thank goodness. I like Michael a great deal. I think he's good for Ken. Maybe love's back in bloom, along with my garden? Ah, well. We can hope.

I hope enough springs will heal Ken's heart. He deserves to be happy.

Don't we all?

Love, Paulie

The following pages are from the incomplete comic of Chapter Nine of Circles.

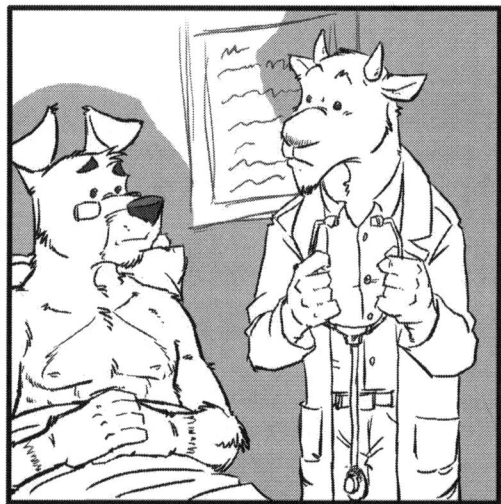

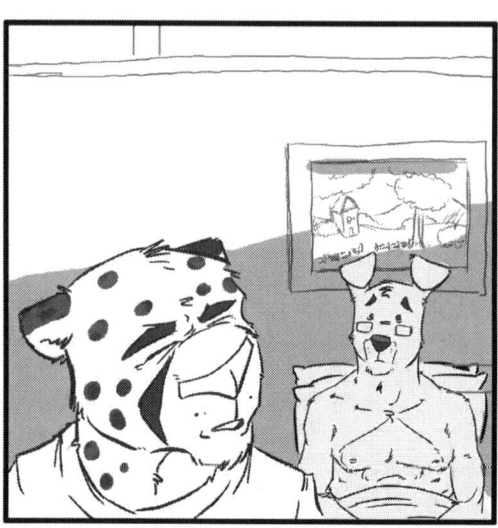

Chapter Ten, Part One: In Your Wildest Dreams

Dear Douglas,

For the first time in I can't remember when, everything seems tremendously peaceful and calm in the house. So why am I waiting for the other shoe to drop?

It's been beautiful to watch the relationship between Ken and Michael blooming as it has. As I'd thought, Ken took the time to tell Michael everything. He opened up, and let someone in, and he's been rewarded for his trust. The two of them are often sleeping over one another's house. Michael's sleeping over here tonight.

Ken's admitting to thinking of me as his father seems to have done something for me, as well. I find myself feeling much more relaxed around Jason. The two of us are getting along famously. It doesn't hurt that he seems to have discovered a love for gardening. He has a real knack for it, too. Clearly something he got from his mother's side of the family, given how bad at it you are.

Just teasing, love. I know you didn't mean to kill those tomato plants.

Marty's been missing Taye, of course. It's hard to watch him deal with that. At least Taye got a weekend off, so we have all our boys under one roof for a change.

Even now, I can see you mumbling something as you roll over in bed, and you have a big smile on your face. You must be dreaming. How sweet! I think I'll join you.

Pleasant dreams, my love.

Love, Paulie

Summer 2003

Ken walked down the street. He couldn't remember what he'd been doing tonight, but he recognized the place ahead. Paradise Island, his favorite place to drink, dance, and cruise the night away. With a grin and a nod to Marc, he slid past the line at the door and into the warm, welcoming embrace of darkness, punctuated by pin-spots in various shades of colored light. The pulse of some new dance piece gave a constant background beat of *untz*untz*untz*, and Ken fell into the rhythm, swaying his ass deliberately with each step.

This was his domain, and he was king here. He had prowled these waters like a hungry shark for years, looking for prey. When he found what he wanted, he grabbed hold, shook it until all the good bits fell out, and then left the remnants behind, hardly caring for the consequences. Why should tonight be any different?

There was something nagging at the back of his mind, but he couldn't quite place it. He decided not to worry about it and plunged into the dancing mob, barely visible as anything but geometric patterns made of people which shifted with each pulse of light. Ken became part of the design, admiring the way that the lights broke everything into moments. He watched against one wall, made up of many small mirrors, breaking the whole dance floor into a complex mosaic.

"Hey, boy," said a voice. He turned, seeing Bo… or was it Uncle Davis? He wasn't sure. They were so alike, in their way. "Where you been? You haven't forgotten that you belong to me, have you?"

"No, I don't… I don't belong to anyone," Ken spat back. He shoved his hand out, a knife suddenly in it, and slashed. BoDavis' head felt back and off. It had just been a cardboard cutout of him, he realized, and he laughed. All around him, there was a party going on. Everyone was wearing masks, and each mask was the face of someone he'd been with. There was poor Joe, over there. A good-hearted guy with too much money, a lack of good sense, and a hard-on for a gym-body physique. There was Cliff. Total hottie, with an awesome sportscar, which somehow he was wearing on a necklace. There was Roger; they'd had a little fling after Taye had broken things off. Roger was kind of a pity-fuck, if he were being honest with himself. All around him were names and faces, but they were all just people in masks. None of it was real.

Except Michael. Michael was really himself. He was standing there, and the crazy mosaic dance pattern swirled around him, looking increasingly Byzantine. For some reason, Ken didn't want Michael to see him. If he had a mask, it would be perfect, but no one seemed to want to lend him one. So finally, he reached down and picked up BoDavis' cardboard face from the floor. He poked out the eyes and held it over his own face, walking up to Michael. "Hey there, Boy. You look lost."

Michael shook his head. "I'm looking for my boyfriend. Do you know if he's here?"

KenBoDavis laughed, a little harshly. "Boy, I ain't sure if he's anywhere at all."

• • • • • • • • • • • • •

Marty was at his graduation. He was in the nude, other than his mortarboard, and he stood up in front of a class in a stadium that was about ten times the size of the one he thought Boston University actually had. He was handed his diploma, which looked suspiciously like a bag of shrimp chips (Taye had brought some back from San Francisco, and he'd had a violent allergic reaction. Even now, he thought his hand was swelling up like a balloon.) Now he had to make his way along the line of teachers and well-wishers. Since he had to shake every hand, and his other hand had his diploma, he had no extra hand to hide his nudity with, and this was causing him equal amounts of frustration and embarrassment.

Dean Halley shook his hand, leaned forward, and murmured, "Congratulations, Mr. Miller. By the way, your genitals are below average in size."

"What?" Marty asked, stumbling along to the next well-wisher, whom he thought was Paulie, but didn't look anything like Paulie.

"Hello, dear," said not-Paulie. "By the way, I'm sure Taye doesn't mind that you're a barely adequate lover at all."

"Th-thanks," Marty stammered, feeling increasingly awkward.

John and Arthur were next, standing together like one being made of two. As he approached, they/he pulled him in, fondling him all over. "We've wanted you since day one," the John/Arthur being said. "We've wanted you, and you've wanted us."

"But… but… Taye," he moaned, softly, feeling how exciting this was.

"Taye will be away for many months yet," John/Arthur told him. "We would like to fill in for him," Arthur's voice said, as John's face kissed him. "Literally," John said, as Arthur's nuzzled his ear.

Marty woke up with a startle, panting in the darkness. He heard Taye's voice next to him, groggy. "Teddy Bear? You okay?"

Marty blinked, the dream already fading from his mind. "Yeah, I had a really weird erotic dream. I can't remember what it was about, though."

Taye chuckled, rolling over, spooning up behind Marty, putting an arm around him. "Well, as long as you're awake, it'd be a shame to spoil all this… excitement."

Marty grinned, rolling over to meet his lover in a kiss.

● ● ● ● ● ● ● ● ● ● ● ● ●

John looked around, realizing everything was in shades of black and white. He adjusted his fedora, shrugged deeper into his suit, and trudged on beneath the grayscale cross-hatching of a street-light's dim glow.

This case is getting to me, he thought. *If I don't figure out who stole the briefcase with Professor Nickleson's formula in it, those secrets could get into the wrong hands. God only knows what'll happen then.*

He trudged on, past buildings, until he came to the door he was looking for. Behind it, a small army of penguins was dipping black-and-white cookies. He sampled a few cookies and tasted newsprint. He looked down and realized he was standing in front of an old printing press, wearing an apron smudged with black inkmarks in the shape of his own hands. He pulled the lever on the press, sending the machine whirring to life, huge cylinders spinning. The text on the newspaper was completely illegible, but he knew it had something to do about the Battle of Pearl Harbor.

He knew he was dreaming. He always dreamed in black and white, and he could never read text in his dreams. And with that realization, he woke up. Arthur was still peacefully snoring next to him, and he smiled, laying back down. Weird dream. He dozed back off again, drifting along on the tides of the subconscious.

• • • • • • • • • • • • •

Jason ran along the beach. He wasn't sure why his Dad and Uncle Paulie to had decided to take him to a nude beach, but he was sure glad to find that it was co-ed. All around him were beautiful women, completely nude. He recognized Becky Barbarino from his Trig class laying out on her back, sunbathing, although she was already incredibly tan, a lack of lines showing that she must always sunbathe nude. She had the most beautiful breasts, and he always loved to think about them during the day. She wore the most incredible sweaters and t-shirts, and they showed off just enough.

Now, however, they were bare, and he moaned, softly, admiring them openly. She must've heard him, because she pushed down her shades. "You like me, don't you, Jason?"

He groaned, kneeling down next to her. "Oh, God, yeah. I like you so much! I can't tell you in school, because I'm afraid you'll tell me you don't like me, or your girlfriends will laugh at me."

She smiled at him. She was so gorgeous. He wanted to kiss her so badly that it made him ache, but he didn't dare. She smiled and rolled over, exposing her back and rear. "I need more suntan lotion. Will you rub it in?" He groaned again, taking the lotion, rubbing it into her gorgeous skin. "Mmmm. You have such soft hands. Rub more."

He didn't need to be told twice. He rubbed more, almost panting with lust. Just then, the tide came up around them, and Becky was just a sand-castle that he was building. A tiny car rolled out across the sand-castle's drawbridge and hit him smack in the groin, causing a strange feeling.

Jason woke up with a groan. He was on his stomach on the couch, and… oh, man… he could feel that he was somewhat warm and damp across his lap. With a grimace, he lifted himself up. At least his pajama bottoms had caught the majority of it. How embarrassing. "Aw, man," he muttered, as he peeled off his underwear and pajamas. He stashed them in the hamper, down below his other clothes, then he made his way to the bathroom, feeling sheepish, to clean up. This was the third night in a row…

• • • • • • • • • • • •

Michael was in a hall of mirrors. He didn't remember coming to a carnival, but he assumed that's where he was. He wandered around, feeling his way along, not trusting his eyes. The mirrors sometimes showed him himself, and sometimes showed him Ken's face, which was odd. He and Ken were getting more and more settled into the idea of being a couple, but they weren't much alike. Why did he keep seeing Ken's face?

He got the idea of leaving a trail to find his way around the maze, but he didn't have anything to use. Finally, he reached down, tugging a part of his hip away. No one would miss that. His hips weren't all that exciting. He walked along, tearing the piece of hip apart, leaving a trail of crumbs behind him like bread. Eventually, he had to tear off another chunk, and slowly, but surely, he made his way through the maze, leaving bits of himself behind. Ken would be at the center of the maze, he was sure. He hoped he'd have enough of himself to get there.

• • • • • • • • • • • • •

Taye fell back, exhausted from a bit of fun with Marty. His chubby lover had already dozed off again. He smiled, wishing he could thank whatever crazy erotic dream Marty'd been having. Whatever it was, it had gotten his Teddy Bear good and riled up; it was kind of rare that Marty was good for twice in the same night, and they'd played before sleep.

Taye thought about dreams. They were funny things. He rarely remembered his dreams at all, but they were usually silly little vignettes. He never remembered the classic falling dreams, or underwear at school dreams. He'd remember little dreams about meeting a talking dog, and being really amazed that a talking dog existed, until he realized that the talking dog was pretty dull to talk to, at which point he'd lost interest.

Taye began to doze, snuggling up to Marty, who was always nice and warm. He didn't dream, that he could exactly recall, but he did remember stepping forward into a gray light, as if a curtain were parting in front of him...

• • • • • • • • • • • •

Arthur walked through a lush green landscape, a rain forest that towered overhead and ran on as far as the eye can see. Birds in intense hues of red, blue, and yellow (macaws, he thought) glittered like jewels on the branches of trees, or whirred through the air like winged rainbows.

He was barefoot, and, with each step, the forest floor grew riotous with streamers of green vines that put forth blooms of many colors that then faded away and offered up thick-skinned fruit that looked and smelled like blue mangoes. Little dancing insects played on the wind like dust motes, or maybe they were faeries, dragonfly wings a scintillating blur.

Arthur made his way towards a place where sunlight was streaming down in a glade. It had only one tree at the center, and that tree was sad, dark, and still. Its bark was a withered grayish-brown and smooth, almost like it had been polished. Its roots were partly exposed, and it was leaning at a desperate angle. No leaves, blooms, or fruits decorated its limbs, which were as bare as if it were winter, and all of the birds and insects (or fairies) stayed clear.

As Arthur got closer, he saw that the area around the tree's roots was bad. The vines and creepers his footsteps had been leaving slowly withered in the parched earth and faded, and finally, even the withered vines stopped appearing. It took much longer than he'd guessed it would to cross the open space to the tree, and he put his hands on the smooth bark, trying to will it back to life.

A noise from above caused him to look up. High up in the branches, numerous children were laughing and talking to one another, their strange language like bells on the air. If the dying tree collapsed, or fell over, he thought, the children might fall. "Climb down!" he cried up to them. "Or jump to other trees!" But they looked down at him and laughed a chattering laugh. This was their tree, their whole world. If it fell and took them with it, so be it, but they wouldn't desert it. He knew he wouldn't, either, and he wrapped his arms around the tree, hugging onto its slim trunk.

"I'm sorry, Paulie," he whimpered.

• • • • • • • • • • • • •

Doug was driving the sportscar as fast as he possibly could. He was dimly aware that everyone he loved and had ever loved – Paulie, Jason, Linda, Kathy, Mrs. Nussbaum, and just everyone – was somehow stuffed in the trunk. It didn't seem to be affecting his driving performance, however. The car was handling beautifully.

He screeched the tires as they rounded across a borderline painted on the ground. He was dimly aware that this meant that they'd crossed the border into Connecticut, but the landscape was dry and dusty, with tumbleweeds going by. The incongruity of this didn't occur to him. It was what it was. He was incredibly dry, thirsty, and he stopped for a drink at a bar by the side of the road. His Evel Knievel-style white jumpsuit with red and blue stripes punctuated with stars was offset by the aviator helmet and goggles he was wearing. For some reason, a necktie with baby ducks on it was strapped Banzai-style around his forehead.

The bar was cool and dark and smelled oddly of mothballs. There was no one immediately in evidence, and now he was aware that there was an old jukebox playing. He walked over, past dusty and disused billiards tables, and dropped a quarter into the jukebox. It began to play a song. He couldn't recognize the tune, but the lyrics seemed strangely important.

Outside, he saw a state cop looking over his car. He stepped outside. "Excuse me. Can I help you?"

The state trooper looked oddly familiar, with a tall, brawny body. He was wearing mirrored sunglasses, like they always wear in movies, but Doug could see some kind of bandage under the trooper's left eye. "Is this your car?"

Doug nodded, feeling suspicious. "So? It's legal."

The trooper shook his head. "You should've checked local laws. You can't transport people across the state line in the trunk like this," he said, nodding to the rear of the car. "It's going to have to be towed and impounded."

Doug felt a wave of nauseous fear grip him. "But you're going to let the people out first, right?"

The trooper shrugged. "I only care about the law. Nothing says I have to let them out."

Doug was shaking. "But they'll die! They need air, and food, and water."

The trooper nodded to where a tow-truck was already beginning to haul the sportscar away. "You should've thought of that before you got all high and mighty." He sneered, getting on his motorcycle. "Maybe your fancy lawyer friend can help. If you can figure out which impound yard they get towed to." The cop gave him the finger, and Doug found himself running down the road, following the tow-truck, but it was soon out of sight. "No!" he screamed. "Paulie! Jason! I'll find you!"

He looked around, finding he was alone, in an empty desert that stretched in all directions, with no sign of a road, or a bar, or anything. How could he find them, if he'd lost himself already?

● ● ● ● ● ● ● ● ● ● ● ● ●

Paulie was sitting under a beach umbrella. It was very peaceful here, with no other bathers in evidence. The tide kept sliding back and forth just a short while away. He knew he was at Bournemouth, so the island he could see out in the bay was the Isle of Wight. He'd been here on holiday as a boy with Aunt Bettina, once. He had gotten badly sunburned, but he'd also had a delicious ice cream with wafers. This was a lot like that day, hot and bright, but the umbrella was keeping him cool.

The tide crept in closer, and began to puddle around his toes. Crabs were scuttling through the little pools, tickling his feet, but he wasn't concerned. He had wonderful news to share with Doug, when he came over. He had met a vacationing doctor who had traded him his ice cream for a diagnosis, and he'd told Paulie what he'd longed to hear for years. He wasn't sick any more. Something had worked, and he was going to be just fine. And he and Doug and Jason would stay together as a family with Taye and Marty and Ken and John and Arthur and Michael and Mrs. Nussbaum, and everything would always be fine, and no one would be sad because of him any more.

● ● ● ● ● ● ● ● ● ● ● ● ●

Paulie awoke with a start. He realized that the noise he'd been hearing was Douglas, moaning, next to him. He reached out, embracing his lover, who stilled and then opened his eyes. "Oh, man," Doug said. "I had the worst nightmare. It was so frustrating. I was lost… and I couldn't get to you, and…"

"Shhhhh," Paulie said, softly, stroking the face and hair of the man he'd loved for nearly fifteen years. He knew every feature of that face, so dear to him. "It was just a dream."

He was aware he'd been dreaming, too, but the details were lost to him. He decided not to worry about it. Dreams weren't truths, after all. He kissed Doug and held him, stroking his hair. "Just a dream," he repeated, wondering why the thought made him suddenly sad.

Chapter Ten, Part Two: Why Can't I Sing It Too?

Mrs. Nussbaum crossed Kinsey Circle, a luscious applesauce-spice cake with caramel icing on the plate she carried. She'd learned the recipe from Mr. Douglas Pope, he of the many wisecracks. But she wasn't going to number 6 to show off her improvement to the recipe (she'd candied pecans and used them instead of walnuts.) Instead, she was bringing it to number 1, the home of Carter Allen and his family. The fact that she was bringing a cake she'd learned to make from her favorite gay household only made her grin a little wider. That would make it sweeter still.

For months now, Carter had been dodgy. He had been making comments about organizing a Kinsey Circle beautification committee. Josie Allen had connived to get her e-mail address quietly added to the list when Carter sent out the invitation to today's meeting. She wondered what kind of beautification Mr. Carter had in mind; she thought the neighborhood was beautiful enough already.

Carter's expression when he opened the door was priceless. "Oh... Mrs. Nussbaum. Um... hello."

She smiled, winningly. "Ach, please, Carter, with us, it is first names, yes? It's Esther, here. And with me is also coming a very nice cake for the meeting. It has the most tooth-aching sweet caramel frosting you will ever taste."

"Caramel frosting? Awesome!" This came from Seth, the older of the two Allen boys, who appeared at his father's side in the doorway. And she heard Charlie, the younger boy, echo, "Awesome!" from inside.

Carter stood there, staring at the cake a bit, and then at her. "The meeting... yes... of course." He looked like he'd been caught with his hand in the cookie jar. He still didn't make a move to invite her inside, or let her pass.

Suddenly, Josie was there, behind Seth. "Oh, Esther, hello. Ooo! That cake smells wonderful. Here, let's get that on the table. You didn't have to bring anything."

Mrs. Nussbaum smiled as Carter found himself being gently edged aside by his wife. She entered, bearing the fragrant cake, enjoying the smiles of the two

Allen boys. She was very fond of them both, and she had enjoyed babysitting them for many years. Lately, Jason Pope, Doug's son, had taken up a bit of the slack for her. She was no longer so young that she could run around after a pair of pre-teens. One barely a pre-teen, she reminded herself. Seth was turning twelve in just a couple of months.

She set the cake down on a placemat Josie pointed to, and then smiled at the others present. She knew all of them, very well. There was Robert Post and his wife Sylvia from number 2. Everyone knew he was cheating on her with a younger woman, and everyone included Sylvia, who seemed more relieved not to have to spend time with him than anything else. Jerome Hochstead lived alone in number 4, and he was a quiet, stay-to-himself sort of man. He didn't have any wife or girlfriend, but she had seen several deliveries from Victoria's Secret come to his house. Mrs. Nussbaum suspected what that meant, but she didn't feel it was really her place to comment on anyone's lifestyles. Finally, there was Anabel Reilly from number 7. She was a funny, raucous woman who probably drank a little too much and talked a little too loudly, but Mrs. Nussbaum adored her, just the same.

"Is everyone here?" she asked, sitting in a comfortable chair that she suspected Carter might've been planning on sitting in. "Ach, but obviously not. None of the boys from 6 are here, and if anyone knows anything about beautification of a neighborhood, it's them. An oversight, this. We should maybe call them? I have their phone numbers in my purse. I'm sure that Paulie or Doug would be..."

"That's alright, Esther," Carter said. "This is just an informal meeting. I don't think we need everyone here in the whole neighborhood."

"Really?" she asked. She looked around with exaggerated movements, then looked at Allen rather pointedly. "Everyone in the whole neighborhood is here, except for them, so what's going on?"

Carter looked a little flustered. He was rescued by the doorbell. "Who on earth is that?"

Josie nodded. "Oh, you said we should have someone sit for the kids. Adult talk and all that." She looked at Seth and Charlie. "Go get your money boys. You're going out to the Science Museum."

Amidst cries of "Sweet!" and "Awesome!" the Allen boys dashed for their rooms. Carter turned back and looked at Mrs. Nussbaum. "Wait. But Esther usually sits the boys, so who…?"

Mrs. Nussbaum smiled with a warmth that she was not altogether feeling. "Don't worry, Carter. I made a recommendation, of course, and someone your boys already know."

Josie opened the door to reveal the short, slight form of Jason Pope. "Hi, Mrs. Allen. Here to pick up the boys."

"Jason, thank you so much for coming by. Won't you come in?"

He stepped awkwardly into the home, looking around. "Oh, hi, everyone." He spotted Mrs. Nussbaum and smiled more broadly. "Thanks for the reco, by the by, Mrs. N. I can use the extra dough. Father's Day coming up, and I have double-present duty."

Mrs. Nussbaum chuckled. "For me, it's also a help. This way, we can have good, adult talk without damaging innocent ears."

Carter was clearly not pleased. "Um… I didn't realize…"

Jason smiled. "Don't worry, Mr. Allen. I've sat for the kids with Mrs. Nussbaum lots of times."

Carter's displeasure was growing. "Oh, good. Well, thank you, Jason."

Jason nodded. "Not a big deal at all, Mr. Allen. They're good kids. No trouble."

Seth and Charlie returned. "Oh, cool! We're going with Jason? Thanks, Dad!" said Seth.

Charlie hugged his Dad. "Thanks, Dad!"

Carter patted his younger son's head. "You're welcome, boys" he said, as if it had been his idea. "Make sure you behave for Jason."

"We will," they chorused. And, with a flurry of checking of details and vanishing boys, they disappeared out the door, with promises from Jason to check in by phone regularly.

Carter frowned after they were gone. He lowered his voice a little. "Honey, I'm not sure I'm comfortable with this."

"Oh, Carter," Josie chuckled. "Jason's a good boy. He's very responsible."

Carter frowned. "He's been in trouble at the school for fighting."

"For defending himself, I think you mean, Carter," Mrs. Nussbaum said, as casually as if he'd been addressing the room. "You know how boys are. Better, I'm thinking, than I do."

"Oh yeah," said Angie in her broad, Boston accent. "That can't be easy for the poor kid. His Dad's gay, and his mom's recently deceased, and…"

"Well, that's kind of the crux of this whole situation," Carter said, finally settling for a folding chair. "Is everyone here comfortable with the situation at Kinsey 6?"

Everyone was quiet for the moment, then Sylvia Post said, "The situation? You mean… Jason fighting?"

"No," Carter said, annoyed. "You know what I mean. We have a nice, normal neighborhood here, for the most part. But that house is like a flophouse for gays. What are there, nine of them living there now?"

"Oh, Carter," Josie said, rolling her eyes.

Mrs. Nussbaum pretended to count. "Technically," she said, "there are six. John Brockhurst, with the bookstore, and Michael Lang, with the ears, do not live there, and Jason, although he lives there, is not gay. At least, not that I'm knowing, and we are pretty close. He tells me about this girl at school named Becky…"

"Not the point," Carter said, rubbing the bridge of his nose with two fingers like his head had started to hurt. "The point is they're always coming and going. I can't keep track of who's who over there."

Now it was Mrs. Nussbaum's turn to roll her eyes. "Oh, come on, Carter. Five of them have lived there since you first moved into this neighborhood with your very nice family. "Number six moved in over two years ago. Yes, there are boyfriends, and now Jason, but it's not like you need a chart to keep track of them."

Mr. Hochstead spoke up a bit quietly. "And what is there to be worried about? They're all very nice men. I think they do a wonderful job of keeping the neighborhood beautiful. Mr. Mayhew's garden is always so bright, and the lights they put up at Christmas…"

Carter sighed. "Alright, do I really have to be blunt about this? I'm not comfortable raising two boys in a neighborhood with six to eight fags living in it. There. Period."

Everyone was shocked. Finally, Josie spoke up and said, "Really, Carter, you're being an ass. I'm not any more afraid of Seth and Charlie being around any one of those men than I am of them being around Mr. Hochstead, or Mr. Post. And, even if I weren't, it's not like we can make them leave."

Carter paused, frowning, then spoke slowly. "Are we so sure about that? I don't know how many people that house is zoned to have living in it permanently. And I'm sure there's at least some pot being smoked in that basement. I've called the cops, but apparently Mr. Mayhew is allowed to use marijuana medically for his condition, so..."

"Really?" Mr. Post said. "This is what we're here to talk about? Zoning violations? Pot smoking?" He shook his head. "Paulie Mayhew and Doug Pope are good men. When Sylvia was sick in the hospital, they came over every couple of days with food, and I know they visited her as much as I did."

"Probably more," Sylvia muttered under her breath.

Mr. Hochstead looked down at his feet. "Mr. Dooley got me a great table when I visited his restaurant. And Mr. Martin helped me recover important... things from my hard drive when my computer crashed."

Angie smirked at the proceedings. "You can't expect me to want them gone. Arthur painted that beautiful landscape on my garage. It fixed up a real eyesore. And Ken and Doug took part in that track and field fundraiser that Kathy from the next block organized for the homeless shelter."

"Again, not the point," Carter groaned, feeling like this meeting was spinning out of his control. "I'm not saying that I think they're fundamentally bad people. But what they do in bed..."

"Isn't really any of our business," Sylvia said, pointedly, her husband shifting uncomfortably.

"Is immoral," Carter finished, as if he hadn't been interrupted. "My church is horrified that they're here."

"Well, I'm horrified we're even having this conversation," Mrs. Nussbaum finally said. "Immoral. You know what's immoral? Hate. Prejudice. This is immoral. Those boys are all good boys. Good people. Anyone who thinks otherwise is full of it, including your church, and mine, for that matter," she said, as he raised a finger. "That's why my church does not see me much, any more. When I meet my maker, I want to be proud about how I've lived my life."

Carter shook his head, sighing. "Look, Esther, everyone knows you're fond of the boys. I don't think you understand how hard it is to deal with this."

"Don't I?" she said, her eyes flashing behind her glasses. "Well, let me tell you something, Mr. Ever-So-Condescending Allen. I understand very well. Have you met my grandson, my Joshua?"

Carter nodded. He knew Joshua. Mrs. Nussbaum's grandchildren played with his boys when they visited, which was fairly often.

"Joshua has a lisp," she said. "It's not because of his teeth. Buck-teeth run in the family, but lisping never has."

"I don't see what this has to do…" Carter began, but Mrs. Nussbaum cut him off.

"No, I don't imagine you do, so I am going to explain to you, and you are going to hush and let me do so."

Carter was taken aback, but he closed his mouth, feeling like he likely had no choice but to listen.

"Joshua lisps," she said again. "He lisps, and he has a slight body, and eyelashes that're just a little too long. And he likes to play with the girls, instead of the boys. And he's just ever-so-slightly effeminate, some would say. Sensitive, I call it. And so he gets teased, in school. He gets called a homo. A faggot. A sissy. He gets pushed around, and beaten up. And he has very few friends that aren't girls."

She tapped her finger on the arm of the chair. "I'm sure you did it, Mr. Carter Allen," she says. "I'm sure you made fun of boys that lisped. You called them queer. Boys do that. Bullying seems to be very natural for boys." She looked at Post, who was looking at his feet, a bit shamefully, maybe remembering something. Hochstead was listening intently. She doubted he'd ever pushed another boy around in school.

She rounded on Allen again. "And do you know what I found out? What my Joshua... my precious grandson did?" She leaned forward. "He tried to kill himself. He locked himself in the bathroom, and he took a bunch of sleeping pills. And he lay down in the tub and tried to drown."

The room was still. No one said a word. No one breathed. "My Joshua did that, because he's just *perceived* as being gay. No one knows if he is or not. I think yes, but his mother thinks no. It doesn't matter. The point is that, being teased and bullied and beaten up for being *perceived* as gay was enough to make him do this. This precious boy, who is the light of my life. Who plays trumpet in band. Who gets straight A's in school. Who wants to be a veterinarian when he grows up, but who cries when he sees animals being hurt in movies. This precious boy was almost lost to us, because of people like you, Carter Allen."

Carter swallowed. He didn't know what to say. Part of him wanted to protest; this wasn't what this meeting was supposed to be about. But Mrs. Nussbaum was still going.

"And now, you want to do that same kind of bullying to my boys at Kinsey 6. You want to make things uncomfortable for them. You want to try and drive them out of this neighborhood, when they *are* this neighborhood. You want to crush something beautiful because it scares you, because you are a small-minded, ignorant man." She rose to her feet. "I don't know about the rest of you, but I think I see a clear path to how to make this neighborhood a more beautiful place." She patted Carter on the arm as she walked past him. "You want to make this neighborhood more beautiful?" She glared down at him. "Then move out."

No one said anything as she made her way to the door. Josie stood and opened it for her. Mrs. Nussbaum looked at her friend's sad, shocked face. "It's okay, Josie," she murmured. "I think he can still be a good man. Maybe we'll see soon, yes?"

After she left, there were some quiet discussions about other ideas for beautifying the neighborhood. Someone suggested a rosebush for the center of the circle, and others mentioned a block party for the 4th of July... although everyone agreed that the boys at Kinsey 6 should be brought in on those plans, as they were the masters of the block party. Everyone left, until Carter, who'd said nothing, was alone with his wife.

"Do you agree with Esther?" he wondered, as his wife cleaned up the coffee cups.

"That we should move? No. I like it here, Carter."

"No," he said, troubled. "About Paulie, and Douglas, and the rest."

She sat down beside him. "Do you remember when you fell off that ladder, trying to hang Christmas lights?"

He nodded. "You took such good care of me. You made that amazing chicken soup of yours, and you paid our bills out of your poker night money."

She shook her head, softly. "That was Doug's soup. He came over with some every day. And Paulie covered our bills. I didn't have nearly enough in the poker kitty."

Carter stared at her. "Why didn't you tell me?"

Josie smiled. "They asked me not to. They know what you think of them, Carter. They're not stupid. I've paid them back the money over the years, of course, but I don't think I can ever really pay them back." She leaned in, and kissed him. "Do you really think what they're doing is immoral, or are you just reacting to what they said at church?"

He frowned. "Reverend Heater was looking right at us when he said it."

She shrugged. "He's an idiot. I think we should try that Unitarian church down the street. It's walking distance, and I hear they have amazing pot-lucks."

"You want to change religions because of pot-lucks?" he asked, incredulously.

"I want to change churches because of hate," she said. "Christ told us to love each other. I don't remember him putting qualifiers on that."

He frowned. "Leviticus says that homosexuality is a sin."

She snorted. "It says that about eating lobster, too. Doesn't stop you when we go to Gloucester."

"But what about the writings of Paul? He clearly says…"

"Honey," she said, softly. "I know what Paul says. Remember which of us went to divinity school. It doesn't mean I have to agree with him. I can believe in God and Christ and not believe that someone in the Bible is right. Paul had a lot to say about slavery and about women not speaking in church, too. How can you expect me to not believe that he's outdated?"

Carter was quiet for a while. Finally, she kissed him again. "You're a good man, Carter. I know change is hard, but the world is changing. It's a different place than when we were kids. Time to change along with it." She smiled, standing up. "Now, if you'll excuse me, I'm going to take a bath without fear of being interrupted by our sons." She started up the stairs, then paused. "Charlie lisps, you know. He might grow out of it, or not." She shrugged, and continued up the stairs.

He sat there for a time, thinking about a lot of things. Had he been someone who bullied sissies in school? He wanted to say no, but he knew that he had. He had to. One time, someone had seen him and Timmy Ross in the shower room. It had all been innocent curiosity, of course, but you had a choice in that kind of situation. Take the abuse, or dish it out. And he had dished it out, starting with Timmy Ross.

He thought about Timmy… wondered where he was, now. They'd been best friends, but that had ended the first time he'd looked Timmy in the face and called him a queer. He wondered if Timmy was gay, or if it had just been curiosity for him, too. He wondered about his own son, Charlie. He'd noticed the lisp, of course, had tried to help his son correct it. Most likely it was just a childish lisp. Lots of kids have one, he thought to himself. They outgrow it, but some don't. What would he think if Charlie told him, one day, that he was gay? He didn't know.

Jason brought the boys home a couple of hours later. They'd spent their allowance money on Omni movies, a planetarium show, astronaut ice cream. Charlie had purchased a stuffed T-rex he had named Rexy, and he showed it off to his father, smiling his gap-toothed smile.

Carter framed his son's face with his hands, smiling. He kissed Charlie's cheek and sent him up to show Rexy to Mom, while Seth was cutting a piece of cake for himself. Mrs. Nussbaum had left it behind. "Ah, Jason. Thanks so much for looking after the boys."

Jason smiled, the lick of his hair down over his eyes as usual. He brushed it out of his face. "No prob, Mr. Allen. They're a lot of fun to hang out with, really."

Carter looked the teenager over. There was nothing effeminate about him. He seemed like a typical teen, a little awkward and gangly, but making his way through life, and hormones, and fear of the future. "Well, I appreciate it. Here." He took some money out of his wallet, offering it to the boy.

"Whoa!" Jason said, brushing his hair out of his eyes again. "Are you sure, Mr. Allen? That's a lot of money."

"I'm sure," Carter said. "I insist." He gave a slight smile. "Double Father's Day duties, like you said."

Jason smiled. "Yeah. Tell me about it." He took the money. "Well, thanks, Mr. Allen. Call on me anytime. I know Mrs. Nussbaum's not always around." He turned to go with a wave, the screen door slowly closing behind him.

"Oh, Jason..." Carter half-stepped out of the door, himself, onto the stoop. "Do me a favor? Tell your Dads I said... um... thank you."

Jason stopped, looked confused. "Thank you? For what?"

"Oh... Josie... my wife... Mrs. Allen. She told me about some things that happened a ways back... I guess I've owed them a thank you for a while now."

"Oh." The teen shrugged. "Sure thing, Mr. Allen."

Carter stood in the doorframe, watching the boy cross the circle, heading home. Then he ducked inside. Seth was sitting at the kitchen table with his cake and a glass of milk. "Hey, Seth, you like hanging out with Jason, huh?"

Seth smiled, nodding. "Jason's awesome. He's really funny, and he taught me how to throw a wicked curve ball."

"Good, good," Carter said, sitting down with his son. "You know about his... um... situation at home?"

Seth cocked his head. "Situation? You mean, like how his Dad's with another guy?"

"Yeah, about that," Carter said, frowning. "Does it bother you at all?"

"Why would that bother me?" he asked. "His Dad's gay, right?"

"Ah, yeah..." Carter agreed. "That's... that's why he's got two Dads. That isn't weird to you?"

Seth shook his head. "Nope. Why would it? It's got nothing to do with me, I guess." He looked at the cake. "You want some, Dad? I took too big a piece."

"Sure," Carter said, and Seth stood up. "Do you want to show me that curve ball tomorrow?"

"Yeah!" Seth said, lighting up. "It's really cool!" He headed upstairs, and Carter watched him go. It was a different world. His sons would grow up without fear of things that he considered different. And he wasn't sure if he thought that was a bad thing or not.

He reached out and picked up a stray piece of the cake and ate it. It was different from when he'd had it before. But it was good. The nuts were pecans, which he liked far more than walnuts, and they seemed to be buttery and candied.

"This is good cake," he murmured, picking up a fork and digging in.

Chapter Ten, Part Three: There's a Lot of Us Running Around

His name was Barry Middleton, but everyone called him Midge. It was a bit of a misnomer; he wasn't a small man. At almost six foot and close to two-hundred and fifty pounds, he was anything but small. He would've qualified as a bear in the gay community, but he didn't have a lot of body hair. He was in his mid-forties, and he'd cultivated a beard and moustache that might have been called sparse, if one was being kind.

Despite this, or maybe because of it, Midge was a really likeable guy. He had a big laugh that was incredibly infectious, and he had a generous nature. He had a collection of extremely loud Hawaiian shirts that he was very proud of, and he loved to wear them down to the clubs on Landsdowne Street, or over to the gay hang-outs in the Theater District or the South End.

Tonight it was Landsdowne Street. They were having a "Boys Night" at Paradise Island, a club that was pretty open to begin with. Every once in a great while, he got lucky. Sure, it was usually someone he wasn't that excited to go home with, but he got by okay. The way he figured it, he was lucky to get lucky. Beggars, choosers, that kind of thing. He still put on his favorite Hawaiian shirt, one covered with a riot of colors and patterns formed by images of tropical drinks.

Once inside, he headed up to one of the higher up levels with a smaller dance floor. He liked the one on the second floor, because it had some nearby tables and its own bar. Heading up there, he found that there was a decent crowd, but he was able to find one unoccupied table. Next to it was another table with two men sitting at it. One was shorter, younger, with dark, messy hair and a pronounceable chubby build, wearing a simple t-shirt and jeans ensemble. He was kind of cute, Midge thought. If he scored with him, he could feel pretty good about his night. The other man was older, blond, wearing a button-down shirt with a sweater vest over it, and slacks. He had glasses, and he was kind of thin. There was a hollowed-out nature to his face that made it look like he might have been sick lately.

Oddly, the two didn't seem to be flirting with each other, or anyone else, despite sitting at the same table. Instead, they were watching the people on the dance floor. Midge couldn't blame them; there were some hotties out there, tonight. Two, in particular, were dancing fairly close to the edge and were easy to watch. The shorter of the two was a little stockier and had dark hair cut short. He was wearing a blue button down shirt with the sleeves rolled up and a pair of black jeans. The taller man was lighter of complexion, with a long, slender body. He was rocking a tank top and white denim jeans outfit, and he was hot enough to pull it off. His ears were pieced in several places.

Midge leaned over to the two observers. "Hot couple that pair, huh?"

Both men turned around and looked at him. "I should say so," the older man said with a wink and a smile. Midge caught a bit of a British lift in the fellow's voice.

"It's too bad the hotties hook up with each other, isn't it?"

Both men looked surprised, then the younger one said, "Uh... yeah, I guess?"

Midge came over, sitting between the two men, since they didn't seem that interested in each other. "I'm Midge, by the way."

The younger man seemed a little irritated by the fact that he'd made himself at home. Maybe he'd interrupted some flirting. "Marty," he said, shaking hands.

"Paulie," the older man said, smiling warmly. "Now, you were saying?"

"Oh, just that, at clubs like this, the hotties tend to hook up, and the rest of us kind of get left on the sidelines. I have a theory about that, though."

"Now, wait a sec," Marty began, but the older man stopped him.

"Now, now, Marty, I believe we should let Mr. Midge have his say." The older gentleman smiled, again. "Go on, Mr. Midge. I am most intrigued to hear your theory."

Midge had his in. He'd been invited to speak, so he plunged into his well-rehearsed theory. It had gotten him laid, now and then.

"Well," he said, "the way I figure it, it's nature trying to go on its normal course, even though there's no point to it."

Marty frowned a bit. "How do you mean, exactly?"

Midge went on, undaunted. "Well, we're gay, right? So there ain't gonna be any procreation when we do it together, right? But nature, she don't care. She makes it so that the pretty ones in the species try to get together, right? That's why jocks and cheerleaders hit it off in high school. Survival of the hottest, right? Nature taking its course."

"Ah, and you think that, for example, these two hotties dancing over here..." Paulie gestured at the two they'd been watching. "They're trying to hook up because, at some instinctual level, they want to breed and produce more hotties?"

"Exactly," Midge said, with a smile. "So where does that leave us, huh? The heavyset? The older? The not so good looking? Well, we just have to buddy up and make the best of it, huh?" He turned and grinned at Marty.

Marty stared at him, and then blinked. "Oh, wait... you... oh, heh..." He rubbed the back of his neck. "That's... sort of flattering? Sort of? But I'm not... uh..."

Midge waved a hand, effusively. "Not to worry, buddy. I get it. Not quite resigned to the survival of the hottest theory. Well, you're young. You'll learn. I'm sure Paulie here knows what I'm talking about, am I right, Paulie?"

Paulie looked almost painfully bemused. "Well, I'm not sure what level of merit I see in your theory. One supposes that there would have to be experiments. Controls. All in the interest of science, of course."

Midge roared with laughter. "Science. Man, Paulie, you're alright. Can I buy you a drink? Just a friendly one, you understand."

Paulie smiled. "Alas, I'm only drinking ginger ale tonight, Midge, and I'm on my last one, as I was planning on heading home soon."

"Ah, too bad," Midge said. "You're a funny guy." He turned to Marty. "How about you, Marty? You want a beer or something?"

"I'm good," Marty said. "Actually, I have to be going soon, too."

"Oh," Midge said. Maybe they were together, after all? "I'm sorry if I interrupted or something. I just figured, where you weren't sitting next to each other..."

"Wheeee!" said someone, and Midge looked up as the taller hottie from the dance floor flopped down on Marty's opposite side. "I love that song. It makes me want to move it, move it. Mm-hmm." The hottie leaned in and kissed Marty on the lips, and it was clear from the depth of that kiss that this was no casual moment. "You ready to go, Teddy Bear?"

"Very," Marty said, standing up, eyeing Midge.

"Um... I think you're in my seat." Midge turned towards the voice and found the shorter hottie standing next to Paulie, arms folded, frowning a little.

"It's alright, love," Paulie said as he stood up, stretching and wincing a bit, as joints popped. "We were just telling Mr. Midge here that we had to go, and offering him our table."

"Oh. That's okay, then." The shorter hot guy leaned up, kissing Paulie as deeply and lovingly, if not more so, than Marty had gotten kissed.

Midge stared at all of them. It seemed so patently unfair, somehow. But Paulie leaned in and patted his shoulder. "Let me offer a counter theory. For everyone in the world, there is someone else who completes them. Sometimes the trick is in being patient enough to find the right one." He straightened up and put his arm around the shorter hottie's shoulder, and the four friends walked off together.

A new song started, and a selection of various other hotties resumed gyrating on the dance floor. Midge watched the others go, then turned to watch the dancers. He was thoughtful. "Anything from the bar?" asked a voice, as a light hand touched his arm. Midge looked up into a pair of baby blue eyes under a blond bowl cut. The young man wore a warm, smiling expression and the traditional attire of a Paradise Island server, sleeveless t-shirt with the club logo and ever-so-tight jeans.

Midge smiled up at him. "Well, that depends. Are you available?"

"Ha, ha," the young man said, his face passive. "Haven't heard that one a million times."

Midge gave a lopsided, apologetic grin. "Yeah, well, you know what they say... million and first time's the charm."

The young man laughed, and it sounded sincere. "You're funny."

"No, I'm Midge." The bigger man extended a hand, and the server considered it, then smiled. His handshake was warm and firm.

"Nice to meet you, Midge. I'm Stuart." They both held the handshake for a moment longer than necessary. Then Stuart smiled again. "I like your shirt."

"Stuart," Midge said, with a smile, "have you ever heard the theory that there's someone out there for everyone?"

The young man shook his head. "Nope." Then he smiled, and his smile was dazzling. "But I'd love to hear about it. Maybe over coffee sometime? I'm working, and this place is loud."

Midge nodded, and slips of paper with phone numbers were exchanged. Midge watched him go, and then looked back at the dancers. They ebbed and flowed like a multi-colored tide under the ever-changing pin-spots, but Midge was only seeing baby blue.

Chapter Ten, Part Four: Walking This High Road

"But I'm not tired," whined Charlie Allen. "I don't want to go to sleep."

Jason Pope shook his head. "You know the rules. Your parents set the times. I'm just the enforcer." He folded his arms and did a semi-credible Arnold Schwarzenegger impression. "I am da Sandman. Sleep, or I will be forced to sedate you with these." He flexed his skinny arms, spoiling the 'illusion.'

Charlie giggled, despite himself. "You're such a goober." He folded his arms. "Anyhow, you can't make me sleep."

Jason sighed. "No, that's true. But I can make you stay in bed. And you'll fall asleep eventually." He made faux hypnotic gestures with his hands, looking into Charlie's eyes. "You're getting sleepy. Soooo sleepy."

Charlie giggled again, then he tried to bargain. "What about a story? If you read me a story, I'll try to go to sleep, I promise."

"Hmmmm..." Jason rubbed his chin, pretending to ponder it. "Well, okay. One story."

Charlie almost bounced in place. Jason was a good storyteller. He did all the voices, and explained the words you didn't understand. "Awwwwwesome!"

Seth Allen poked his head in. "Are you telling him a story? Can I sit in?"

Jason nodded. "Sure, man. Pull up a floor."

Seth sat cross-legged on the floor while Charlie snuggled down under his Spiderman comforter. Jason smiled and began. "Once upon a time..."

"Hey," Charlie said, dubiously, "you didn't get a book out or anything."

Jason shook his head. "Nope. I'm going to tell you a story that you won't find in any book... because it's a true story."

"I dunno about that," Charlie said. That made him suspicious. "Is it going to be a cool story?"

"Hey, Doubting Doofus," Seth said with a snort. "How about you listen up? If you don't think it's cool, you don't have to go to sleep, okay? I wanna hear Jason's story."

Charlie weighed his options, then waved his hand. "Continue."

Jason rolled his eyes. "Thanks so much for your confidence in me. Now, as I was saying… ahem…" He closed his eyes and started again. "Once upon a time, there were two knights. They had been questing in far off lands, they were returning home, and they were weary from the road…"

• • • • • • • • • • • • •

"I can't believe I let you drag me all the way to Dorchester," Arthur snorted. "Now we have to take the T all the way back. It'll be, like, midnight before we get home."

Doug laughed. "You lazy ol' thing. I can't control where the fundraiser is. Besides, admit it, you enjoyed playing with the kids."

"Being mauled by them, you mean," Arthur snorted. "Those kids play rough."

"All joking aside, man, I owe you," Doug said with a little smile. "A lot of those kids… they don't come from such happy situations. It means a lot to them to have a little attention from someone."

Arthur smiled. "Aw, you know I'm just grousing, Dougers. I like helping you with these. And Kathy's hugs make trekking out here all worthwhile."

Doug nodded. "That woman hugs like she means it," he agreed.

• • • • • • • • • • • • •

"The two knights, weary from their long day of questing in the name of good and right, were making their way to their home kingdom. As they did so, however, they heard a cry of distress."

"Was it a damsel?" asked Charlie. He liked to be sure of these things.

"Of course it was a damsel," Seth snorted. "You never read stories about a dude in distress."

"Some dudes need help too," Jason assured him. "And these knights did not discriminate in the aid they gave. But in this case, yes, it actually was a damsel in distress."

"Told you," Seth said, rolling onto his back on the floor. From that vantage, he couldn't see Charlie stick his tongue out at him. Instead, he imagined the two knights, clad in shining armor, riding their horses towards the damsel, who was probably in a tower…

• • • • • • • • • • • •

"Was that a scream?" Doug asked, nervously. "Did you hear a scream?"

"I heard something," Arthur said, feeling his whole body go tense. "C'mon! Someone might need help."

Doug shuddered. "Whoa, whoa, whoa! Hey there, Superman. Shouldn't we call the police?" But Arthur was already sprinting towards where the scream had come from. "Oh, Jeez," Doug said. He pulled out his cel phone, and he was thumbing 911, but he couldn't seem to get it to work right.

Around the corner, they found a man and a woman struggling over her purse. "Just let it go, you stupid cow," the man growled.

"Hey, asshole!" Arthur yelled, rushing towards the pair. "Hands off!"

Both man and woman looked shocked, but the man recovered first, yanked the purse out of the woman's arms, and ran as fast as he could. Doug didn't blame him. Arthur was a big guy, and he looked pretty scary when he had his angry face on.

• • • • • • • • • • • • •

"The damsel was being attacked by a terrible robber. The satchel she was carrying held something very precious to her, and she didn't wish to lose it. With faces set in a fearsome aspect, the two knights challenged the robber, rushing to the aid of the damsel. Alas! The robber wrested the satchel from the damsel…"

"What's 'wrested'?" Charlie asked.

"It means that he got her purse… I mean satchel," Jason explained.

"Oh." Charlie lay back. "Did they gallop their horses after the robber?"

"They didn't have horses. They were afoot."

"What?" Seth looked up. "That's bogus. If they were knights, they should've had horses. Even the word chivalry comes from a French word that has to do with horses. I learned it in history class."

Jason sighed. "Look, the knights were on foot. Knights don't sit on their horses all the time, you know. How could they get in a bathtub, or go to a nice restaurant if they had to stay on horses."

Charlie giggled. "It's funny to think of a knight, on his horse, in the bathtub."

"That's right. So can I continue, Mr. Vocabulary?" Jason asked Seth.

"Sure, whatever," Seth said, closing his eyes. He'd just have to edit the horses out of his mental picture. No biggie.

"Now, as I was saying, the knights were afoot. After ascertaining that the damsel was not injured, they gave pursuit to the robber, for she told them of the precious treasure within her satchel, and they wished to return it to her.

● ● ● ● ● ● ● ● ● ● ● ● ●

"Lady, are you okay?" Doug asked, running up beside Arthur. He'd finally gotten 911 dialed properly, and he hit Send, waiting for the line to answer.

"It's just a purse," Arthur told her. "Not worth getting hurt over."

"But you don't understand," the woman sobbed. "My Pumpkin was in there."

"Your what?" Arthur asked, confused.

"My dog!"

"Aw, shit. I… okay. Stay here. I'll get your Pumpkin back." Arthur sprinted off, after the figure they could still see under the streetlights.

Doug goggled as he ran. "Arthur, I… aw hell." He tossed the phone to the woman. "It's 911. Tell them what's going on. I'll grab my phone back in a minute." He pelted after Arthur as fast as his legs could carry him.

Arthur was taller, however, and had a long stride, if not the most athletic build. He was rapidly catching up to the man. "Drop the purse, you fucker!" he growled. "It's got her dog in it!"

The man, short and wiry, with a shaven head, suddenly turned, a knife appearing in his hand. "Yeah? Too fuckin' bad, man." The man looked bad, like he hadn't slept, or eaten in a while. Crackhead, Arthur guessed. He'd seen a few since starting to work around the homeless shelter. He'd probably sell the dog for money, given a chance.

Doug came up a little more slowly, assessing the situation. This was bad… stupid bad. Why were they chasing down a purse snatcher in Dorchester at eleven at night? He saw the glint of the knife in the man's hand and swore under his breath, then crept up, trying to approach a bit more stealthily, in the shadows of the buildings…

"The knights met with the robber, and he drew his sword, giving both of them pause. They feared this blade, for it seemed to glitter with a malign light."

"That means it looked bad," Seth told Charlie.

"I knew that!" Charlie said, although he hadn't.

"Didn't they have their armor on?" Seth asked.

"Indeed they did," said Jason, "but the sword looked perilous, as though it might be enchanted with a wicked spell, so they approached with caution. The two knights slowly split up, trying to get on either side of him. One raised his shield..."

• • • • • • • • • • • •

Thinking to distract the robber, or at least knock the knife out of his hand, Doug picked up the lid off of an aluminum trash can. Arthur was circling to the guy's left, so Doug came in from the right. The man heard him coming and slashed with the knife, but Doug managed to swat it with the trash can. He didn't drop the knife, but it deflected the blow and distracted the man.

Arthur came in fast — faster than Doug expected. The man whirled, and the blade flashed, but Doug's fist connected with the guy's jaw with a bone-crunching thud, and the man fell.

"Ow," Arthur said, clutching his hand. "Think I broke my hand on this asshole's chin."

"That's not all," Doug said, going pale, watching an inch long wound in Arthur's side oozing blood.

Arthur looked down at his side. "Oh..." He felt woozy, all of a sudden. "Ain't that a bitch." He sat down hard, on the curb, looking a bit sick and faint.

• • • • • • • • • • • •

"One knight took a blow from the dolorous sword on his shield. The other knight rushed in and struck the robber a blow on his helm that rendered him senseless, but, in doing so, he was wounded."

"Oh no!" Charlie said. "Was he okay?"

Jason nodded. "Thankfully, the blow, although it had cut through his armor, was not deep. He had to have several stitches, though."

Seth peered at him suspiciously. "Stitches?"

Jason ignored him, plunging ahead. "Although they were wounded and more weary than ever, the two knights waited to make sure the damsel was safe and returned her satchel of treasure to her."

• • • • • • • • • • • • •

The woman came running up to them. "Oh, my God! Are you two okay? The police are on their way."

"Hopefully they'll bring an ambulance," Arthur muttered.

Doug picked up the purse, offering it to the woman, who almost cried gratefully as she opened it up. Inside, as she'd said, was a small purse dog. "Oh, Pumpkin!" she sobbed. "I was so scared I was going to lose you. The little dog yapped and wagged his tail as though nothing had happened. "Oh, how can I thank you guys."

Doug looked down at Arthur, who groaned. "Tell you what… make a donation to the shelter down the street, and we'll call it even."

She smiled. "I know just the one you mean. I absolutely will. Thank you both so much." The police were arriving shortly thereafter, and the woman was giving her statement.

Doug sat down next to Arthur as the police were calling in an ambulance. "You were awesome, man. It was mythic, watching you go."

"I don't even like those kinds of dogs," Arthur muttered.

• • • • • • • • • • • • •

"The end," Jason finished.

Charlie looked at him suspiciously. "It was true?" he asked.

Jason nodded. "Totally true."

Seth looked over at Jason, then at Charlie. "He's talking about when the ambulance came with his Dad, remember?"

Charlie nodded. "Your Dad and Mr. Arthur stopped a robbery, right? Is that what the story was about?"

"That's right," Jason said, with a smile. "Now you can tell people you know two knights."

"Awesome," Charlie said. He snuggled down into the blankets, thinking about it.

Jason and Seth left the room to let Charlie try to sleep. "That's pretty cool that your Dad and Mr. Arthur did that," Seth admitted.

"Yup." Jason had been super-proud of his Dad since he'd heard the story.

"So, even though they're gay, they just did really brave stuff?"

Jason shrugged. "What does being gay have to do with it? Being gay is just about the kinds of people you love, not whether you're brave, or good, or smart, or anything like that."

"I didn't mean it that way," Seth said, defensively. "It's like… on TV, the gay characters are all prissy. I couldn't imagine them chasing a robber or anything."

"Well, my Dad and Mr. Arthur aren't much like those gay people on TV, now are they?"

Seth thought about that, and shook his head. "No, they aren't." He thought a little longer, then said, "Mr. Taye is a little bit like those people."

"A little bit," Jason said with a grin. "But you'd better not let him hear you say that."

• • • • • • • • • • • • •

"You're an idiot," John said, looking scared and angry at the same time.

"The police said so, too," Arthur said, laying back in bed with a wince.

"Well, they were right. A total idiot."

"I know," Arthur said, closing his eyes. "It was stupid. But I just hate people who take advantage of other people, you know?"

"Yeah," John said, trailing off. "Besides… it's kind of hot."

Arthur peeked open an eye. "What? That I could've died?"

"No, you jerk," John said, carefully sliding into bed next to him, trying not to jostle his side. "That you got all heroic and stuff. What you did was stupid… but it was really brave, too."

Arthur chuckled. "I'm not sure how to respond to that in a way that won't sound either falsely modest or completely egotistical. So I'll just say thank you."

John curled up with his lover and smiled. "You're welcome," he whispered.

• • • • • • • • • • • • •

Paulie had been white as a sheet when they came home. He wasn't much better now. "You can't do these things to me," he whimpered.

"I know, Paulie, I know," Doug said, soothingly. "It won't happen again."

"Don't say that," Paulie said, firmly. "I know you. You're as bad as Arthur is. Worse, because he's huge and can wrestle an omnibus, if needed. What if something had happened to you? What am I supposed to do then?"

Doug opened his mouth... and then closed it again. He'd almost said, 'What I'll do when you're gone,' to Paulie, but there was no level on which saying that would be fair. "I'm sorry," he said instead.

Paulie sighed, a long exhalation, letting tension go. "It's okay. What you did was really noble." He sat on the bed, shirtless, a number of emotions at war within him. Finally, he let out a nervous laugh. "All to save a purse dog?"

"Don't get me started," Doug grumbled. "Probably a good thing that we ran after him, though. Dog might've ended up over a campfire or something." He snickered. "Roasted Pumpkin."

Paulie groaned. "Very nice. So does your little heroic story have a happy ending?"

Doug grinned, sitting next to his lover. "And they lived happily, ever after."

"Ever after's a long time," noted Paulie, thoughtfully.

"Okay, then," Doug said. "They lived happily for... whatever after."

"That works," Paulie said, holding his lover in against his body.

A moment later, Doug looked up at him. "Wanna mess around?"

Paulie grinned. "Thought you'd never ask."

Dear Douglas,

It's been a funny sort of summer. There haven't been any big, defining moments that I'll remember, looking back, except, perhaps, for the heart-attack you gave me from chasing after that purse-snatcher.

Things seem to be fine. Mostly everyone's together, and we're all enjoying spending time as a family. I feel for Marty, though. With Taye still on the road 95% of the time, his apartment must be very lonely. I've been making it a point to invite him up whenever possible.

Carter Allen even seems to be warming up, and Mrs. Nussbaum said something about a guerilla tactic spicecake. Occasionally, I wonder if even Mrs. N. knows what she herself is talking about half the time.

Maybe life isn't really about the big stories. The important events can tell you something about a person, but it's how we go through life in the day to day that really make up the stories of our lives.

I hope that this chronicle of both the large events and the day to day will be something you'll be glad you have. Down the road, as it were.

I love you, Douglas. You'll always be my hero.

Love, Paulie

Chapter Eleven: We Have to Pay for the Love We Stole

Dear Douglas,

The days are growing shorter, and that crisp autumn air is in the offing once again. It's been a good year, so far, and I hope we cruise easily into 2004 with no major drama.

Taye is coming back in a few weeks. Poor Marty's been missing him rather terribly. Lacking school over the summer to distract him, and with only a part-time job so far, I think Marty's going the relationship-equivalent of a little stir-crazy. He's been playing a lot of Dungeons and Dragons with his other friends, but it seems like he's still in need of more affectionate companionship.

Luckily, Arthur seems to have somewhat stepped into the void. He's been bringing Marty along on art projects, having Marty pose for him. The two of them have gotten quite close, which is good. Marty can use a good role model like Arthur, I think.

Jason is starting back to school, and we hope that the new year doesn't bring any repeats of the trouble last fall. Jason seems like he's made friends, but it must still be tough trying to explain about having a gay Dad and losing his Mom.

I hope we made the right decision bringing him here. He's had some tough times in his life, and I just hope we haven't made things any tougher.

I think we did. I think what we did was what was best for both him and you.

I think I'm coming down with something. I feel run-down, and kind of achey. Maybe I'll try to take it easy so I can get better and enjoy the rest of the year.

Here's to a fine autumn for all of us.

Love, Paulie

Autumn 2003

Doug studied the surface of the pancake with a surgeon's eye, watching for the first tiny bubble that would tell him that the side touching the griddle was perfectly golden brown. He prided himself on his pancakes, as he did on every recipe that he found the proper formula for perfection with. Doug liked things precise, things that could be dropped into neat rows and boxes, quantified and calculated. It made him a natural at accounting, and caused him a lot of anxiety when things were outside of his control.

He looked over at Paulie, chatting away at the breakfast table with Marty. How could their relationship ever have worked, he sometimes wondered. It was the antithesis of the orderly and perfect world of numbers. Life with Paulie was messy, and he normally hated things that were messy. The craziness with Linda, Jason's problems at school, a lover who was HIV positive… these were not orderly and calculated things.

But that was his life, and he relished every moment of it.

"I hate every moment of it, Paulie," Marty sighed. "I feel… it's like an ache. Like I feel so unfulfilled without him." Marty blushed brightly as he thought of how that might sound. "I… I don't just mean the sex… though that's really rough, too. I mean, with Taye gone, I just don't know what to do with myself. He's always the social one, the one that gets us out there and active. I mean, don't get me wrong, I'm still playing D&D with my buddies, and Jesús has been great, trying to distract me with tango lessons… but I need Taye to be back. How did you stand it when Doug went to Maine?" The chubby young man rubbed the back of his head, self-consciously.

Paulie chuckled. "I knew he'd be back, dear. And I had my journal, and all of you." He reached out, patting Marty's hand, then picked up his tea cup, sipping it. "You must be excited. Just a couple of weeks to go, yes?"

Marty groaned and fell back against the sofa. "Don't remind me. Weeks. Oy. I am going to kiss him so hard when he gets back. But he says the tour's been going really well, and the director really likes his work. This could mean more acting jobs for him." He sat forward again, frowning. "That could mean more tours… more stretches where he goes away."

Paulie studied his young friend's face. "Are you… having second thoughts about your relationship with Taye? It wouldn't be the first time distance interfered with romance."

Marty's expression was almost panicked. "Second thoughts? God, no! I love the heck outta Taye. But… this is just hard. I knew what I was doing was right when I told him to go. I just didn't know…"

Paulie smiled. "Marty, dear, if you love Taye, you'll both find a way to make it work. You should talk to him about it. Maybe… well, I don't know how Taye feels about it, but if you want to encourage him to act more… well, Boston's theater community is good, but you know New York's is better."

Marty frowned. "Move away? I don't like that idea so much. I mean, after college, I want to get a job, save some money, and do some traveling with Taye, maybe in Europe. But move? I really like living here with you guys, Paulie."

Paulie's smile warmed and widened. "And I love having you lads in the house. But we can't all live together forever, you know. There are… it just can't be."

Marty frowned more, but Doug's appearance with the pancakes interrupted that train of thought. "No more gloomy talk," Doug said, firmly. "Pancakes. Butter. Syrup."

Paulie chuckled. "Yes, dear." He poured the heated syrup slowly, watching it melt the little yellow pats of butter.

Doug turned back to the stove, frowning. Paulie was clearly more frail than he had been even a year ago, and, although he stayed cheerful, little morbid comments like that one kept cropping up, too frequently to be inadvertent. *We can't all live together forever.* Doug bit his lip. If… when he lost Paulie, how was he supposed to deal with that? Marty might miss Taye, but Taye would come back.

Doug washed the griddle with damp paper towels while it was still hot, studying the water droplets as they beaded up, sizzled, and steamed. Could he stay when Paulie's health really went downhill? Could he handle that? And yet… how could he ever leave?

Doug frowned more deeply and ran his fingers under the water in the sink, thinking about the future.

• • • • • • • • • • • •

"Hey, Pope, how's your two faggot fathers?"

Jason felt his hand clench into a fist, involuntarily, and stared at the locker in front of him for a moment. He knew who it was without turning around. Chris Wilson. P.E. was the only class they shared, but every time they were in the locker room together, Wilson had been going out of his way to provoke him. Now, it seemed, that abuse was crossing over into the regular school hallways. No wonder he'd already been in two fights only a few weeks into the first semester of High School. Jason had been warned by the principal not to get in any more fights, and he wondered if Wilson knew that.

He turned around, looking the squat, broad-shouldered boy in the eyes. "My Dads are awesome," he said. "Thanks for asking. How's your Mom? According to the football team, she's great."

Wilson stared at him. "Why would the football team say... ?" Realization dawned on the boy as kids around him sniggered. "I'll fuckin' kill you!"

"Not today you won't," said a deep, authoritarian voice. "Beat it to class, Wilson." It was Mr. Bukowski, their P. E. teacher. Lucky bit of timing, that. "And Pope, stop antagonizing other students."

Jason's eyes widened. "Me? He came up to me and started hassling me about my folks!"

Bukowski regarded him unsympathetically. "Yeah? Well, maybe you need to grow a thicker skin, given your... parents."

The fist he had started to open clenched again. "Are you sayin' it's okay for him to say things like that?"

Bukowski shrugged. "I'm saying you should grow a thicker skin. Your parents are what they are, and people are going to talk about it. If you throw a punch every time someone says something butt-headed, you're going to get expelled."

Jason frowned. Was this good advice? Insult? It was hard to tell. Bukowski noticed. "Just get to class, Pope," he grumbled, and walked off.

Jason turned back to his locker, trying to haul out his sociology books. He felt hurt, confused, unhappy. He tugged, and too many books came out. They fell to the floor, scattering his homework.

"Great," he muttered, as he knelt down. He collected papers, then realized someone was offering him several that had fallen out of his reach. He followed the hand up to the face and swallowed. Becky Barbarino. He'd never actually spoken to her, but, as he accepted the papers, he managed to mutter out a "Thanks."

"You're welcome," she said. Wow! She was sure polite. "Don't mind Wilson. He's a jerk. I think it's cool that you stand up for your Dads."

Jason stood up, brushing his hair out of his face, feeling awkward. "You do? Um… cool. I didn't know you knew about my Dads." That was lame, but, hey, he hadn't even known she knew he existed.

She smiled and shrugged. "People talk. And I have a friend who lives in your neck of the woods. She says they're a nice couple." She plucked a stray end of her hair that was getting in her field of vision. "I should get to class. I just wanted to say I think you're right to stand up for them, no matter what Mr. Bukowski says. Just maybe you should find another way than fighting?" She smiled. "See you in homeroom."

Jason smiled back. "Yeah. Cool. See you there."

Jason watched her go, then headed for class, thinking. The world had just shifted, and new things loomed on the horizon.

● ● ● ● ● ● ● ● ● ● ● ●

"To what do I owe the honor, gentlemen," Paulie said with a chuckle.

John and Arthur had shown up with gifts. Bribes, Paulie suspected. A box of his favorite tea. A fresh loaf of bread. A book he'd been planning on buying from Triangle. He already knew the answer to his own question, but it was fun to play the game with them.

John looked comically aggrieved. "Paulie… Jeez… we're your two oldest friends. We can't come up and offer you some nice things now and then?"

The bread did smell good, he had to admit, but Paulie couldn't help himself but to tease. "Comfort me in my dotage?" He grinned. "Alright, boys. How much?"

Arthur shrugged. "Just enough for a couple of joints. I wouldn't bug you, but my friend who usually hooks me up is out of town, and John and I just want a couple for the weekend."

Paulie shook his head. "Such times are these, when I, a respectable homeowner and philanthropist, should be reduced to the status of a drug dealer."

Arthur laughed and kissed Paulie's cheek. "Oh, come off it. You love it. You love feeling like you're somehow getting one over on the state. We all know it."

The older man chuckled. "Well, I must admit there is something wickedly amusing about it. It's so… so… illicit!"

"Oooo! Illicit! The author pulls out a nice ten-dollar word," John said with a grin. "C'mon and give over, Grandpa. Give us the drugs!"

Now, Paulie couldn't contain the laugh. It bubbled up and burst out of him. "Alright, alright. You villains. Let's see what I can spare. Honestly, I don't use that much of it myself… just when my arthritis is acting up. Makes me ache, and the pot helps, but I just don't enjoy smoking that much anymore. Doug, bless his heart, tries to make brownies with them, but they made even his brownies a tad vile." He opened the small box he kept the medical marijuana in and emptied some into a bag for them. "Here. This is about half of what I have. If I suddenly need more, my doctor's going to get suspicious."

Arthur accepted the baggie. "Many thanks, good sir, for this delightful party favor. Hey, do you wanna pose for me? I always get super in the mood to paint when we're smoking up."

"Perhaps not this time," Paulie said. "I have some projects I want to putter on." In truth, he didn't want to be naked in front of his old friends. He'd lost some weight lately, and he didn't like how he looked. Even with Doug making some of his favorite foods, he just didn't have the appetite he once had. He reminded himself to mention that to Dr. Roberts at his next appointment. Then he remembered. "I know! You should ask Marty to pose. He's been going out of his mind as Taye's return date gets closer. This might help distract him."

"Good call," said John with a wicked grin. "Wouldn't mind seeing that cutie pose naked for you. Maybe a lil of your Medical Maui Wowie will help relax him, too."

Paulie was thoughtful. "I don't know if Marty does that, but you can always offer."

"We'll throw it in as a bonus, not a selling point," Arthur chuckled. "I'll ask him."

"Hey, Teddy Bear," Taye said, leaning against the wall of the hotel room, the phone cradled to his ear. "Just stepped out of the shower. It's so good to hear your voice."

"Good to hear yours, too," Marty's voice came crackling over the line. "So, are you naked?"

Taye giggled. "What is this? An obscene phone call? Yes, I'm naked, and a dozen horny actors are wanting to ravish me."

The voice on the other end of the phone was surprised. "Really?"

"Not really, you goof," Taye laughed. "I'm in my hotel room. And my roommate isn't here right now, thank goodness. He's pushy. And obviously wants me... not that you can blame him."

"No one can blame him, for wanting your bod," Marty sang in a husky voice over the phone.

"Your Bowie needs some work," Taye said. "But that makes me want to watch *Labyrinth* when I get home. And *Dark Crystal*, and every awesome movie ever. I've been watching crappy pay-per-view for waaaaay too long, now." He twirled the phone cord in his fingers. "So whatcha doin'?"

"I'm supposed to go pose for Arthur in a bit, but I really wanted to say hi."

Taye grinned. "So are *you* naked?"

"Not yet," said the voice, with an anxious little tone. "I think John's there, too. Do you think he'll take off while Arthur's painting?"

Taye hmmmed. "You could ask him to if you're not comfortable. John was there when Arthur did one of me. He checked me out pretty thoroughly." He giggled. "He's a horny fella. Quite the voyeur."

There was a long pause on the other end of the phone. "Does that bother you?" Marty finally asked. "I mean... if he were there?"

"Not really," Taye said. "He's an old friend. I've probably been naked around more guys in the last few months than I can count on my fingers. Nudity's no big deal for me. You c'n show off your bod to John, if you want."

"I dunno," the voice said, uncertainly. "I guess I'll see."

"Relax, Teddy Bear," Taye chuckled. "I'm sure John will take off, if you don't feel comfortable."

"It's just weird. I've been naked around you, and Arthur, but not too many other guys. It just feels funny."

"Well, branch out, lover," Taye said, hearing voices in the hall. "I think my roommate might be back, and I *am* naked, so I'm going to grab something to put on. We'll talk soon, okay? Only a week til I'm back!"

"I can't wait that long," Marty groaned over the phone line. "Come back now."

"Soon," Taye promised, and made a kissing sound. "I love you, Teddy Bear."

"I love you, Taye."

• • • • • • • • • • • •

John wasn't there when Marty came in. "He's just out getting some snacks and beer," the artist confirmed. "He'll be back in a bit." Once again, Marty pondered the disconnect between his big, burly friend and the delicate artistic touches in his work. He's seen those huge hands produce tiny brushstrokes with absolute precision. As someone who couldn't draw a straight line with a ruler in hand, Marty envied him that talent.

The big bear of a man was dressed in his overalls, as he usually was when he worked. Marty was wearing only his bathrobe. "So… is he going to be here when you're painting?"

"That's totally up to you," Arthur said with a warm smile. "If you're not comfortable, he'll probably go up and hang out with Paulie."

"Paulie's not up there," Marty said, a slight note of concern in his voice. "He and Doug were going into a Parent-Teacher conference at Jason's school tonight, remember? And I think Ken is sleeping over at Michael's." He rubbed his arm. "It's just the three of us."

Arthur laughed. "Then we'll send John to the movies." He hugged the shorter man. "Marty, John's not going to do anything weird. And if you don't want him here, then he'll take off. He's a cool guy."

Marty chuckled, ruefully. "I'm sorry, I know I'm being a little bone-headed."

Arthur picked up the joint he'd rolled earlier. "Look, we're going to relax. I'm going to smoke. We'll do some painting and posing. And we'll go out for Chinese after. Sound good?" He lit the joint and took a long drag. "Mm… Paulie gets the best stuff."

"Oh… that's' some of Paulie's… ?" Marty looked over. "Jeez, I haven't done pot since high school."

Arthur offered out the cigarette. "You should try it. I promise this is better than any shit you had in high school."

Marty hesitated, then shrugged. "Well, sure… okay. If that's cool?" He came over and took a short drag, then exhaled. Then took a slightly longer one. "I don't even know if it does much for me, honestly. I don't remember anything particularly amazing from high school."

By the time John came in, the joint was half-gone, stubbed out to preserve the rest for later. Arthur was working on a canvas, sketching in lines with the stub of a pencil, as Marty relaxed on the posing sofa with a blissful smile. John paused, taking a moment to look over the chubby younger man's naked body. "Well… I didn't know the party was going to get started while I was away."

Marty startled up, grabbing his robe, and pulling it over himself. "Oh, shit! You scared me."

John averted his eyes politely. "Sorry, man. Didn't know you were down here, yet. I'll just drop the beer in the fridge and then take off if you want."

The blush on Marty's face deepened a little. Taye had told him to relax. To branch out. He felt so awkward… like a little kid. Compared to Taye and Arthur and John, he was so inexperienced and sometimes uncomfortable in his own skin. "I… no. That's cool. I just didn't realize it was you." He slowly let the robe fall, relaxing again. "I mean… hey… you've seen naked paintings of me, right?"

John chuckled. "This is true. Arthur loves painting you."

A slight cough from Arthur made John turn. His lover was shaking his head with a frown. John remembered that Arthur's crush on Marty was not something widely known. He felt embarrassed himself now and stumbled on to cover the fact. "And, hey, you're a cute guy, Marty. Nothing to be ashamed of. No wonder he likes you as a subject."

"You think I'm cute?" Marty asked, blushing even more furiously.

"Absolutely," John said with a grin, putting the beer in the big corner fridge. He grabbed a bowl and emptied a bag of tortilla chips into it, then emptied a jar of pineapple salsa into a smaller bowl. He brought both over to the coffee table within Arthur's reach, then sat down on the empty side couch, grabbing a magazine and looking it over. In truth, he was more interested in looking over Marty, and he stole plenty of surreptitious glances. He'd always liked a wide variety of men's bodies, and he liked the shorter, younger man's curves. He wondered what it would be like to caress them.

"Taye's back soon, huh?" he asked.

Marty nodded, smiling. "Yeah. Thank God. I thought this tour would never end. Who knew that nine months could feel that long?"

John groaned. "Oh, man. You must be so danged horny."

That was not what Marty had been expected, and he blinked, sputtering a moment. "I... well... sure. Of course. You know, it hasn't been nine months straight. Taye did come back a couple of times. But for the last three months... I haven't... y'know..."

John chuckled. "Well, I'm sure you *have*, by yourself?"

Somehow, that struck Marty as incredibly funny, and he giggled uncontrollably. "Well, y-yeah," he managed, between giggles. "I mean... of course *that*. But not... you know... the real thing."

Arthur ignored the chips. He never ate while he was working, though he'd take a break soon to enjoy some, wash the snack down with the beer, and share the rest of the joint. He found himself looking over Marty, slowly, sketching here and there. Not for the first time, he wished he'd been the one asking for a roommate when Marty came calling. He wanted Marty, rather badly. The subject had come up with John, a few times, when they were drinking, and his lover had encouraged him to act on those impulses, but he couldn't imagine doing that to Taye. Taye was too good a friend... too good a person to do anything like that, too.

Still, as he absently listened to John and Marty chat, he had to admit that, between the pot, the conversation, and the fact that the object of his affections was so close, it was difficult to stay calm and focused. He made sure he had the basic shapes sketched in, then put down the pencil. "Break time. I need a new pencil soon."

"Chips," said John, raising them. "C'mon over and grab 'em."

Marty put the robe back on, tying it loosely, and came over, flopping down on the sofa, next to John, as Arthur took some of the offered chips and munched them. In fairly short order, a round of beers had been emptied, and everyone was on their second bottle. The joint was lit, and it was being passed around. "You were right," Marty sighed, half-laying back after exhaling. "This is way better than what we used to smoke in high school."

"Fuckin' A right!" John exclaimed. "I don't know how Paulie always gets the best of everything, but he does." The burly man sat back, too, admiring the way Marty's chest was rising and falling as he breathed.

Arthur did, too. Marty looked so beautiful all blissed out and relaxed, and for one moment, he imagined the three of them in bed together, writhing, wrapped around each other. Then he frowned and shook his head, slowly. "I should wash my hands," he mumbled. "They're all gray on the edges from the pencil lead." He stepped over to his bathroom, closing the door, then gripping the sink. He couldn't deny the ache he felt, the desire to do things with Marty. But how could he ever face Taye if he did? In the back of his mind, he was thinking of Doug and Paulie. Doug had been so angry with him for what had happened to Paulie... blaming him. How could he look Taye in the eye if this happened?

Back in the room, John watched his lover go. Arthur had always been shy and timid. It was hilarious when you considered how big a man he was, but it was true. John knew how deeply his interest in Marty ran, and he wanted to see the artist happy. If it was going to happen, however, it looked like it was up to him. John turned back to Marty. "Can I ask you something really personal?"

Marty blinked, opening his eyes. "Um... I guess?"

"Are you and Taye exclusive, or is it an open relationship?" John asked, cocking his head to one side.

It was a little shocking to have it out in the open like that. "O-open? Um... well... we... we never really discussed it." Marty looked down at his hands. "I mean... Taye gets hit on a lot, but he's always turned them down. But I don't know if it's because we're exclusive or just because he's not interested."

John shrugged. "That's him. What about you?"

Marty laughed. "Me? Well, it's not like guys have been breaking my door down... ever."

"Why not?" John asked, a bit incredulously. "You're a cute guy... I'd date you in a heartbeat... so would Arthur actually."

"Really?" Marty tried to think about that.

John nodded. "If Taye hadn't latched onto you so quickly, I guarantee Arthur would've been right there. He and I probably wouldn't be together now if things had worked out different."

Marty tried to imagine that. He felt suddenly shy for how many times he'd been naked in front of Arthur. He hadn't known his friend's feelings for him. Then he shivered as John put a hand on his shoulder, squeezing. "What do you think about Arthur? Can you imagine being with him? Maybe being intimate with him?"

What *did* he think about Arthur? Arthur was such a sweet, kind friend. He was handsome, too, and very funny. It wasn't hard to imagine being with Arthur. Intimately? He bit his lip. Arthur always wore no shirt under his overalls, and at times, Marty had wondered if he wore anything under there at all. The thought had actually caused him some embarrassing moments during earlier posing sessions, although Arthur had assured him it was natural with guys, no problem. Marty found himself suddenly wondering if Arthur had liked seeing him like that.

John grinned. "So you're not necessarily exclusive with Taye. You like Arthur, and he likes you. Why not kiss him?"

"Kiss him?" Marty blushed deeply. "I... I couldn't do that."

"Why couldn't you? It's not like sex, right? It's just a kiss. Paulie and I kiss hello and goodbye all the time, and you don't see Doug getting bent out of shape."

"That's different," Marty said, frowning, trying to get a good defense going. "That's just friendly stuff."

John shrugged. "Why's this got to be any different?"

Marty rubbed his arm. "If... if I kiss Arthur... I'll probably get... y'know... excited..."

"Oh?" John asked with a laugh. "You're lookin' pretty excited right now."

Marty looked down and blushed. His body was betraying how much he actually did like Arthur. It would be a lie to say that he hadn't been interested in the big artist, and now the evidence was pretty clear.

It was at that moment that the bathroom door opened, and Arthur came back in. He stopped, staring at the pair of them. John patted Marty's back, softly, and gave him a little nudge, causing the young man to stumble towards the artist.

Arthur blinked. "Marty? What... um... ?"

Marty hesitated as he got close... but only for a moment. He leaned in and softly kissed Arthur on the lips, closing his eyes.

Arthur froze, feeling a jolt of naked terror at how things had spiraled out of control this way. In moments, however, that terror was wiped away by an awareness of the softness of Marty's lips, of how his breath tasted of chips, salsa, beer, and pot. He was aware of how painfully and suddenly aroused he was, and his arms went around Marty. He could see and feel how excited the young man in his arms was, and for a moment, he readied himself to let go... to give in...

And then he gently eased Marty back by the shoulders, breaking the kiss. The smaller man looked up, confused, disappointed. "We can't, Marty," Arthur said firmly. "We can't do this to Taye."

A look of horror crossed Marty's face. "I... oh, fuck... I'm... I'm really sorry about this. I should... I should go."

"Marty," John began. "It's cool..." But a snap from Arthur's fingers and the furious expression on Arthur's face silenced him. Marty pulled the robe around himself more tightly, tying it. He turned, an anguished expression on his face, as if he were going to say something. But he bit his lip and left the room, walking hurriedly on bare feet.

"How dare you?" Arthur hissed at John. "That poor kid's head is full of beer and weed, and you decide you're going to mess with him?"

"Mess with him?" John looked stricken. "Jeez, Art, what did you think I was going to do? I know how badly you want him. I just thought... he says they've never talked about being exclusive. I thought maybe this was your chance."

"Oh, and you, of course, would leave, letting us have our fun, then come back like a fairy godfather once our wishes were granted, that it? Come on, John. You wanted a piece of his ass, and you wanted me on board with the plan."

John blinked. "Jesus. You really believe that of me. After…" He shook his head. "I like Marty, babe, I'd do it with him, sure, but you're the one in love with him, not me. I just… I wanted you to be happy."

Arthur flushed. He looked at John's face and saw honest hurt in his eyes. "You really did this for me, didn't you?" He shook his head. "This isn't the 70s any more, John," he said, feeling tired and a little ill. "Just because they never talked exclusive doesn't mean it isn't what Taye wants. And Marty loves Taye. He's horny now, and not thinking right, but if we did anything, he'd never forgive himself." He touched John's face. "John, I know you're doing it for me… but if Marty and I are ever gonna be together, it'll be because Taye's not in the picture any more. Not because I took advantage of him."

John hung his head. "I didn't mean to do anything wrong. I just thought…" He swallowed. "Maybe I should spend the night at my place."

Arthur looked at his lover's face. He knew it so well, after so many years, and he truly believed there'd been nothing malicious or devious in John's intent. Nevertheless, he said, softly, "I think you should."

• • • • • • • • • • • • •

"So, you called us in because… ?" Doug was leaning forward, intense, defensive. In front of him was Assistant Principal Vasquez, a short, balding man with patchy facial hair. He looked tired, unhappy to be having this conversation.

"We're concerned about Jason's proposed extracurricular activity," Vasquez said, a bit nervously. "What he's suggesting is… well, it's never been done at this school before, and we want to make sure Jason's thought through the ramifications."

He glanced to his left, where Paulie was sitting back in his chair, legs crossed, fingers steepled together. Beyond him, Jason was sitting, arms crossed, jaw jutted out a little, defiant. "Is there something against school policy about the group my son wants to put together?"

Vasquez squirmed in his seat a bit, shuffled some papers. "We considered school policies very carefully, and there's nothing that says that a…" He frowned down at the piece of paper in front of him.

"Gay-Straight Alliance," Jason said. "There's no reason our school doesn't have one, except that no one's started one. I've spoken to a bunch of students, and they're in support of it, too."

Vasquez frowned again. "There's nothing against starting a Gay-Straight Alliance, as long as you have a teacher willing to be involved."

Jason smiled, a bit deviously. "Mr. Ripley has already volunteered." Doug was not surprised. Mr. Ripley, who taught chorus, was about as left-wing as they came, and probably delighting in causing anguish to the conservative core of the school.

"Well, then..." Vasquez said, "Our main concern is whether or not Jason has considered the possible backlash starting such a club may have amongst the other students."

"Possible backlash?" Doug found his temper rising. "My son has come home with black eyes, a bloodied nose..." His fists clenched and unclenched slowly. "He's gotten into trouble and fights, all for standing up for the fact that his father happens to be gay. You don't think he understands consequences?"

"And Jason's difficulties are another concern," Vasquez said, looking more uncomfortable. "Several teachers have brought that up as this has been considered. There have been incidents of fighting."

Doug had heard enough. "If this fighting continues, it's because your staff are continuing to let other students make slurs. Your school brags about its vigorous anti-bullying policy. If my son were smaller, this would be bullying. I shudder to think what happens to students here who *are* gay."

Vasquez looked more uncomfortable and unhappy than ever. "Mr. Pope, if it were entirely up to me, I would have no issues at all with this whole situation. I think Jason is a good student, and I sympathize with what's happening with him. In fact, I think this organization could be very good for the student body."

Doug spread his hands. "Then what's the issue?"

"Well," Vasquez sighed, "there are still people at this school who won't be happy this is happening. Students and teachers alike. There are those who won't like one bit the idea of this... gay prom that's mentioned in the proposal. They may protest if we allow our gymnasium to be used for it."

"That's too bad for them," said Paulie, speaking for the first time. "School organizations can't be denied access to facilities in a publicly funded school. It's a violation of the Federal Equal Access Act. The federal court in Utah determined that in 1999." Vasquez, Doug, and Jason goggled at him a moment. The older man smiled. "What? I know how to use the internet."

Vasquez shuffled some papers, then smiled. "I see that you *have* considered this more carefully than I'd realized." He stood, and they did the same. "I'll speak with Principal Kushner and the School Board," he said, shaking Doug and Paulie's hands, "but I can't see any legitimate obstacles to the group forming." He smiled more broadly, shaking Jason's hand. "Well done, young man. Good luck."

As they exited out of the office, Jason laughed and hugged Paulie. "Equal Access Act? Is that real?"

Paulie was surprised, but hugged back, wincing a little at the ache in his back. "Of course it is. I'm not in a habit of lying to school officials, dear. I thought you might need a little ammo, so I did some research. If they set up something more formal, I'll even wear a suit to make sure you get your group."

Doug hugged Jason and ruffled his hair. "I'm so proud of you, Jace. This is… well… it means a lot to me."

"Well, it means a lot to me, too," Jason said, looking up at his father. "It's stupid that people are all gunked up about it. And there are some kids at this school who're getting picked on for no good reason. I want to help."

"And you know we're here to help you," Doug said, as Paulie nodded in agreement. "You're gonna need posters, bake sale brownies, chaperones…"

Jason smiled. "Thanks, Dad." He looked up, then put one arm around each of them to hug. "Dads."

Dads. Paulie felt his heart melt. Jason had never referred to him as Dad before. He looked down at Jason, and gently kissed the boy's rumpled hair. "Thank you, Jason," he sighed, softly.

Jason said, "There is one thing. There's this girl… who's helping me with the club. Could we have her over for dinner sometime? She'd like to meet you guys."

Paulie and Doug exchanged a look over Jason's head – surprise, fear, excitement, joy. "We'd love to meet her," Doug said quickly. "We'll even be on our best behavior."

"I hope not!" said Jason with a chuckle. "That'd be boring."

● ● ● ● ● ● ● ● ● ● ● ● ●

Something was wrong. Taye could tell by Marty's posture, the slightly forced nature of his grin, and the tone of his voice. He could tell Marty was being cool in front of everyone else, as the Kinsey family welcomed him back. Paulie and Doug were the same as always of course. Well, Doug was. He was pouring out glasses of a Welcome Home bottle of his favorite wine, laughing and happy to see him. Paulie seemed very tired, and maybe a little under the weather. Jason seemed more relaxed and comfortable than when he'd left, like he was settling in. Ken was there, which he'd heard about from Marty over the phone, and Michael was there. That was good. He liked Michael; Michael seemed good for Ken.

John wasn't there. That was something else he noticed. And Arthur…

Arthur was there, but he wasn't there. Arthur was terrible at hiding his feelings, but he was great at disconnecting. Arthur hugged him, told him how good it was to see him back, and then… nothing. Arthur sat aside, not asking questions, not telling stories. He'd heard that Arthur and Doug had foiled a purse-snatching, but only Doug told the story.

And then there was the look.

At one point, he noticed Arthur looking over at Marty, and when Marty looked up and their eyes met, both looked… guilty. Taye felt his mouth go dry. Something had happened between them. Something bad. And he was afraid he knew what.

He was fairly sure that Marty was the only person in the house not to realize how Arthur looked at him sometimes. Marty was so naïve, and so inexperienced in so many things. Taye had tried to sound him out about it sometimes, but it was clear that Marty was oblivious to Arthur's interest, and he hadn't shown interest before.

Or had he? There had been little moments… the fact that Marty posed naked for Arthur, when he was so shy otherwise. A memory of Arthur and

Marty dancing together in Paulie's living room during one of the innumerable house parties. They had laughed and hugged. Had it been more than innocent?

But innocent or not, the palpable tension between them now was new. It was different. And Taye didn't like it one bit.

He bided his time, talking with his friends until he felt he could politely excuse himself. The flight from L.A. had been long and tiring, and he was looking forward to sleeping in his own bed. One by one, the others left the apartment, with Arthur almost sprinting out first.

Finally, he and Marty were alone, and Taye looked over at him. Marty was looking down at his feet, looking unhappy. "That's what my Dad used to call a confession face," Taye said.

"Huh?" Marty looked up sharply. "A what?"

Taye frowned, arms crossing over his chest. "He said he could always tell when I felt bad about something and was about to tell him about because of the face I made."

"Oh." Marty tried to force a smile, but he gave up quickly, sighing. "Taye... this... this isn't how I wanted to welcome you home, but... I do have something to tell you."

"Something about you and Arthur?"

Marty winced. "Dang, is it that obvious?"

Taye threw up his hands. "Marty, you two wear your hearts on your sleeves at the best of times. When you feel bad, it's not hard to read you. So... something happened between you two? While I was gone?"

"It... yeah..." Marty put his face in his hands. "I... I didn't mean for it to happen. I was posing for him... and John was there. And we had a joint... some beer... and it just... we just..."

"Oh, my God, John, too?" Taye was shocked.

"No!" Marty protested quickly. "John... John didn't do anything. It was just... me and Arthur." He hung his head, looking unbelievably wretched.

Taye felt sick to his stomach. This was the last thing he had expected to come home to. "Did... did they push you into it? I know how pushy John can be.

He's told some crazy stories about when he and Arthur and Paulie used to run around the club scene."

"Not really," Marty said. "I mean… John kind of pointed out to me that Arthur was into me… but I didn't… I didn't do anything I didn't… want to." He hung his head again, and Taye's heart almost went out to him, despite how wretched this whole situation made him feel.

Despite his desire to comfort Marty, he steeled himself, standing up. "I had so many opportunities on the road," he murmured. "And not once did I take advantage. So many guys… and women, too. They offered, or asked. And I said no, every time, because I knew my… my boyfriend was waiting back at home."

Marty's tears were dripping down his face now, but Taye forced himself to ignore them. "I'm tired," he said, after being silent a moment. "I'm going to bed. I think it would be best if you slept on the couch. We can talk about… anything else in the morning."

He made it into the bedroom, got the door closed, and lay down on the bed, fully dressed. He pulled the pillows in, because they smelled like Marty and wept, bitterly.

Marty sat on the couch, unable to move. This was everything he had dreaded. He wanted to say that it had all meant nothing. It had just been horniness and lack of control. He wanted to say everything Taye meant to him, to protest that they'd never talked about being exclusive. But all he said was, "Fuck," and he said it quietly, to no one.

He hated how bad he was with words, how clumsy. He struggled when he tried to say what was in his heart. He stumbled over what to say when. He wrung his hands, trying to figure out how to make it right. He wished he could go up and talk to Paulie, but Paulie seemed so tired all the time, now. He didn't want to disturb him. But, as he thought of Paulie, it was almost like he heard the older man's voice, offering him advice, and he smiled, slightly. He knew to make it right. Write.

He was terrible at talking, but he was pretty good at figuring things out in writing. If he could just write down what he wanted to say, he might be able to explain everything to Taye.

He pulled over the laptop, opened a new document, and began to type.

• • • • • • • • • • • • •

"So, what do you think happened between Marty and Arthur?" Doug asked.

"Hm? How do you mean?" Paulie asked, slowly undressing for bed.

"Oh, come on, Paulie. You saw how they were acting. How they looked at each other. Jeez… you don't think… they did it?"

"I guess I didn't notice," said Paulie.

Doug blinked. Paulie noticed everything. And his voice sounded so weak and tired. He turned, to see Paulie struggling with the buttons of his shirt. "Paulie?"

Paulie looked up at him, and Doug was struck by how hollow his lover's face was. He reached out, brushing fingers over his forehead. "Jesus! Paulie, you're burning up!"

Paulie hung his head, looking nauseous. "I… I don't think I kept much down today. And I'm aching all over. Probably getting a touch of flu."

"I'm calling Dr. Roberts," Doug said, alarmed. "If you have the flu, then fine, I call him out for nothing. If not…" He let the words hang there a moment. Then he turned, and picked up the phone, calling.

Paulie sat on the bed. He knew it wasn't flu. He had been feeling the aches for some time now, but he'd been passing them off as flu, or arthritis, even to himself. He knew it was more, though. He was dizzy, nauseous, feverish. Something was wrong, and he knew, with a sudden premonition, that this was something new… something worse.

He felt himself falling backwards and was absurdly glad that he was already on the bed. He dimly heard Doug call out his name, and then there was nothing.

• • • • • • • • • • • • •

Taye woke up, still dressed, less than an hour after he'd collapsed into bed. He'd thought he'd heard footsteps going up and down the stairs, but it was too late for that. It must have been the lingering elements of a dream. He reached over, feeling the large, empty space where Marty should be, and then he remembered.

He lay in bed a moment, trying to sort things out. If Marty had strayed, what was next? Was he upset enough to end things? Was this a one time thing? Marty was awfully young, after all. Many young men his age had had several partners, but Marty had only had one, really. Maybe he felt the need to experiment? And, if that were so, was he okay with Marty's decision to do so?

It wasn't as though he'd been around for Marty to ask permission, after all. Was this his own doing, going off and expecting a kid — and Marty *was* just a kid in some ways — to be faithful for all those months?

Finally, it was his bladder that made him climb out of bed. Too much "Welcome Home" wine. He tiptoed to the bathroom, dimly aware that Marty's laptop was open, the glow illuminating the form of his lover sleeping on the couch. Marty had probably tried to drown his sorrows in some MMORPG or another. He was always playing some game. Taye frowned. Maybe Marty just wasn't mature enough to be in a relationship like this. Maybe he'd made a mistake. He had sort of seduced Marty, in his own, slow way, playing little tricks like keeping the beds linked together. Maybe if he'd let things evolve normally...

But hadn't he given Marty all the time he'd needed to decide to be in a relationship with him? He'd never tried to rush the physical part of it.

He sighed. There were too many questions, and he was too sleepy. He leaned over to shut the laptop, and he realized that Marty was writing something. It wouldn't be a good-bye note, would it? Did he intend to sneak off dramatically in the morning? Taye leaned in, reading.

```
Of all the touches we have shared, and may yet
share, there will never be another one quite like
our First Kiss. In the instant in which our lips
met, my heart paused, for just a moment, in its
steady beating, as if to acknowledge the power
of a force which is both bigger than itself and,
suddenly, more imperative to my survival than
even the flowing of my blood. In that instant, I
realized how much I had come to love you, and I
smiled, inwardly, at the revelation that I now
knew the person I wanted to spend the rest of
my life with. I wanted to keep on kissing you,
holding you, standing beside you, and loving you,
until the day I died, and I knew that, on that
```

```
day, my ghost would wait, patiently, on the other
side, until you were there. Because I now knew
that there could be no Paradise unless you were
there.
```

Taye read it, feeling his heart wanting to burst, feeling tears threatening to well up again, even though he felt like he'd cried himself dry. He looked at Marty, who slept curled up on the couch, a blanket half-draped over him for warmth. He touched the young, innocent face, and the soft, dark hair. He slowly wormed his way over, sliding down between Marty and the couch's back, spooning up behind him.

Marty partially woke up. "Taye?" he asked, groggily.

"Shhh," Taye said, softly. "The bed's too big, and I missed my Teddy Bear." He slipped his arm around Marty, and the two of them dropped off together. Whatever else needed to be said could be said in the morning.

● ● ● ● ● ● ● ● ● ● ● ● ●

Arthur sat on his sofa, feeling like he'd been flayed. Right now, he was sure, Marty and Taye were discussing what had happened. He was afraid that one stupid mistake had ruined the relationship of two of his best friends. Marty would never be able to forgive him, and Taye...

He shuddered. He'd known Taye for much longer than Marty. He'd seen the frost that Taye could turn on when he was angry. He'd seen the break-up between Taye and Roger. Roger was all heat, but Taye was all ice. He didn't know if he could handle that ice being turned on him.

A knock at the door froze his heart a moment. Was Taye coming down to confront him? Was Marty looking for a place to sleep? He climbed the few steps to his door and opened it, only to find John standing there. "Um... hey," the other man said.

"Hi," Arthur said, hollowly. "Taye was asking for you. He got home tonight."

"I know," said John, looking over at the door that led to Marty and Taye's apartment. "I didn't think that would be appropriate. I didn't think I could stay cool. I would blow it."

"Oh, I'm fairly sure it's blown," said Arthur with a soft sigh. "I don't think Marty or I did a particularly good job covering up." He smiled, ruefully, then

stepped out of the way. "Come inside, love. I'm not angry or anything. I don't blame you."

John looked visibly relieved as he stepped inside. "Thanks, babe. I didn't mean to hurt anyone. I was asking Marty if they were exclusive. I was just drunk and high and stupid. I know how bad you want him."

Arthur shook his head, as he closed the door. "I know. I know, John. But I don't need to get everything I want in life. I already had you, y'know?"

John bit his lip. "You mean that?" He sat on the couch, looking up, looking more doubtful and uncertain than Arthur could ever remember.

"Course I do," Arthur said, puzzled, sitting beside him. "Why wouldn't I? I love you, you dope."

There was no answer for a bit, then John spoke, slowly. "I... I'm not young... I'm not new, or exciting. I'm an old queen. I had good game back when we all first met. Nowadays, I'm just some guy. Marty's cute, he's young..."

"Shush," Arthur said, leaning in to kiss John's lips. "When I said yes to you when you asked if I wanted to be back with you, I wasn't saying, 'Until something better comes along.' You're not my consolation prize, John. You're my guy." He took John's hand, kissing it. "Remember, you rescued me! You're my white knight."

"Jeez, Art," John said, leaning in. "I just thought... you would always talk about Marty when you got a little drunk. I thought you really wanted him."

Arthur grimaced. "I guess I did talk about him a lot, huh? Well, Marty's a great kid, and I'd be lying if I said I didn't think it'd be fun to tumble him. But I don't want to be with him forever." He grinned, softly. "He's only about half my age. What would we talk about?"

"Ah, I see how it is," John snickered. "I'm old and reliable." He put an arm around the big bear's shoulders, then sighed. "Jeez, Arthur... did we ruin those kids' relationships? Are they gonna be okay?"

"I don't know," Arthur said, softly. "I don't know."

• • • • • • • • • • • •

The flashing lights outside half woke Taye up. He lifted his head, laying it on Marty's shoulder. The combination of red and blue meant ambulance, he thought. Did someone have an accident? The knock brought both of them more fully awake. It was about two in the morning. They stumbled together to the door and opened it. Outside, Doug was struggling into a jacket. "Guys... thank God, I... Paulie's going to the hospital. They can only take one other in the ambulance. Can you guys look after Jason?" Jason was standing on the steps above his father in his pajamas and socks, looking worried.

"Ambulance?" Marty said in confusion. "What's going on?"

"Of course we will," Taye said, realization dawning on him. "Do you want us to come to the hospital?"

"We'll do that," said Arthur. Taye turned and saw their door was open, too. Arthur looked solid, dependable. Whatever had happened was gone from his face, and he was now the friend who would always be there. Taye noticed John was there, too, but it wasn't the time for friendly greetings.

Doug nodded. "Thank you. Just... thank you." The normally strong man's face was crumbling, like a paper mask in the rain. "I... he fainted. He's got such a high fever, and he's aching all over."

Taye reached out, squeezing his hand. "We'll take care of things here. Just go."

Doug nodded, rushed out the door, and the ambulance was soon squealing away, its sirens running. Arthur and John, faces set and grim, followed in Arthur's car.

Above them on the steps, Jason sat down, looking miserable. "I've never told Paulie how cool a guy he is," he said, sadly.

"You'll have plenty of chances to tell him," Taye said, firmly. "Do you want to come in and hang out? I don't think anyone's sleeping tonight."

"No, I..." Jason looked at his hands. "I have some things I want to work on. It'll keep me busy. I kinda wanna be alone."

Marty said, "Well, you know where we are, if you wanna talk, or play video games, or eat some breakfast, or whatever." Jason nodded, stood up, and walked upstairs.

The door closed behind them, and they stood together in the kitchen of the apartment a moment, before Taye turned to Marty with tears in his eyes. "Oh, Teddy Bear," he sobbed, hugging onto him tightly.

"Taye, I'm sorry, I'm so sorry," He was hugging back, clinging, crying openly.

"It's okay. It's okay," Taye said, stroking his hair. "I... I just..." He pulled back a little. "Let's talk, okay?"

A few minutes later, they were settled on the sofa in the living room with tea. The laptop was still open, and Marty reached out to shut it. Taye stopped him, looked over the words again, then smiled. "That's really beautiful... what you wrote."

"I swear it's all true!" Marty said. "What happened, it was stupid, it was a mistake..."

"It's okay," Taye said again. "I guess we should've talked more. I took a lot for granted." He was quiet a moment, and then said, "Do you want an open relationship?"

"No!" Marty said quickly. "I don't... really. There's nothing wrong with that, but it's just not what I want. Taye, I love you. Like, I'm *in* love with you. The stuff with Arthur... I was just so horny, and we... we kissed. And it was a mistake..."

Taye nodded. He was prepared for it now. It was still a dull ache in his heart, but he had just had things put into perspective. "And after you kissed... the rest of it..."

Marty looked down. "That was it. We kissed. I mean... I wanted to do more, I really did. But Arthur was... he was so good. He stopped it, and reminded me of you, and then I felt so dirty... and stupid..."

There was a long silence. Then Taye asked. "You just... kissed?" Marty nodded wretchedly. And then Taye grabbed a pillow off the couch and swatted Marty with it. "You dork! You had me thinking you two had done the horizontal mambo on our bed or something! A kiss?" He laughed, feeling relief flooding him.

Marty sulked. "It's not funny. And I *wanted* to do more. I was totally ready to do more."

"But you didn't," Taye said. "Right?" When Marty nodded, Taye leaned in, pressing his forehead to Marty's, framing the beloved, chubby face in his hands. "Arthur may have stopped you, but you didn't push for it afterwards, did you?"

"No. When he said your name, I sobered right up. But... man, Taye... I was so turned on."

Taye giggled. "Marty, if unfaithfulness was based on boners, the whole world would be unfaithful to each other."

"Heh. Guess you're right."

"Course I am," Taye said, poking his tummy. "In that sense, I've been being unfaithful to you for years. I've gotten excited around some other cute guys. Even some of the guys I was touring with. As for the kiss, well..." He smiled. "I think I can forgive that. Arthur's a pretty lovable guy. I'd probably kiss him, given the chance."

Marty rubbed the back of his neck. "So, are we okay? I'm sorry I didn't explain earlier now. I'm bad with words. I didn't know what to say."

Taye patted the laptop. "You said everything beautifully, love." Then he frowned. "Poor Paulie. Poor Doug."

"Paulie's going to be okay, isn't he?" Marty asked, looking worried. "I mean, he's had fainting spells before."

"I don't know," said Taye, after a moment. "I guess we'll have to wait and see."

● ● ● ● ● ● ● ● ● ● ● ●

Arthur came back to the house a few hours later. He'd come back to grab some things Paulie needed, and a few books in case the stay was longer than anticipated. John had stayed with Doug at the hospital. When Taye stepped out into the hallway as he came in, Arthur paused.

"How is he?" the younger man asked.

"Woozy. They're giving him some antibiotics for the fever. Dr. Roberts is running some tests on him."

Taye leaned on the doorframe. "Do they know what's happening?"

"No," Arthur said with a sad headshake, "but Dr. Roberts doesn't think it's good. I guess Paulie's been feeling pain for some time and has been passing it off as just aching joints, arthritis, the flu..."

"Fuck," said Taye. "Why would he do that?"

"I don't think he wants people to worry," Arthur said with a bitter chuckle. They were silent a moment. "Taye, I..."

Taye shook his head. "It's not the time. Just... Marty told me everything."

Arthur nodded, lowering his head. It took him surprise when Taye stepped in and kissed his cheek. "I'm glad it was you," he said with a small smile. "You're a good friend."

"But..." Arthur was flummoxed. "But we..."

"Kissed. And then you stopped anything else from happening." Taye was matter-of-fact. "I forgive you for kissing him, and bless you for not letting it go further. I love him so much, Arthur. I don't know what I would've done, if..."

Arthur looked down at his friend. "Marty's very special. I'm jealous, but he's all yours. And John's mine."

Taye nodded, smiling. "Keep your hands off mine, and I'll keep my hands off yours."

They hugged, briefly, and then Arthur went in to get what Paulie needed, and the deeper worry set in for both of them.

● ● ● ● ● ● ● ● ● ● ● ● ●

"So how bad is it, Doc?" Paulie said, weakly, smiling. It was their standard joke, ever since Paulie'd started seeing the good doctor, years past.

Dr. Roberts sighed. "It's not good, Paulie." He looked at Doug's worried face as the young man hovered by Paulie's side, holding his hand. Dr. Roberts hated this part of his job, but he knew no one would tell them more gently. "I have more tests to run, but I'm pretty sure you've developed t-cell prolymphocytic leukemia. What they call knobby leukemia sometimes."

All the blood drained from Doug's face. "Leukemia. Jesus."

"It's a rare form," Dr. Roberts said, sadly. "Very aggressive. It can attack blood, bone marrow, the liver..." He trailed off. "I think the pain you've been having is from damage to your bone marrow."

Doug looked nauseous, then made himself feel strong. "Okay, so, how do we deal with it? Where do we go from here?"

Dr. Roberts didn't say anything for a while. "Well, with a healthy patient, I would proscribe a combined chemotherapy regimen. There's no drug that it responds to well, but, sometimes, by combining several, it's possible to combat it. My concern is..." He paused.

"I'm not a healthy patient," said Paulie, softly. "Isn't that a funny term. Healthy patient. Why would you be a patient if you were healthy?" He chuckled, quietly, then said, "So for a non-healthy patient, what kind of prognosis are you giving me?"

There was silence in the room. Dr. Roberts had known Paulie for years. He'd treated Doug, and Jason, and Marty, and all of the Kinsey boys, but he knew their patriarch best. He rubbed the bridge of his nose, pushing his glasses up a moment. This wasn't easy. Finally, he said, "Even with successful chemotherapy, the disease's aggressive nature... it reduces lifespan dramatically."

Paulie didn't seem scared. He seemed resigned. Doug was trembling, though, and Paulie gave his dear lover's hand a gentle squeeze. Finally, Dr. Roberts said, "Months. The median lifespan after diagnosis is about seven and a half months. In your condition... honestly, even if you'd told me as soon as the pains began..." He trailed off again. There didn't seem to be much he could say.

"Not long," Paulie said, softly.

"No." The word hung between them. "Paulie... you should probably get your affairs in order. And I really think you need to come into the clinic... and be prepared to stay."

Paulie sighed. "I hate hospitals," he said, turning his head, looking out the window. The white building angled back sharply, so that his view was primarily of more windows. "But I'll do what you think is best."

"We can try the chemo," Dr. Roberts said softly, then added, "But I don't recommend it. It's costly, which I know is no object, but it's painful, and toxic. We can try it, but I don't..."

"No need to say it," said Paulie, softly. "I can hear what you're not saying. You don't think there's much point. It won't help. It may even speed things along." Doug choked back a sob, and Paulie held his hand as fiercely as he could, wanting to be brave for his love.

"I'll give you two some time," Dr. Roberts said.

When he was gone, neither of them said anything. Doug sat on the edge of the bed, and Paulie stared out the window at the row of identical windows facing him. Somewhere below, he knew, was a nice little park where convalescing patients sometimes sat in the sun. He wondered if he'd sit in that park, from time to time.

"Arthur's... getting you some things," Doug managed to get out.

"Doug, it's alright," Paulie said, softly. "I know this isn't what you signed up for."

"Don't say that," Doug said. "I knew you were sick when we met, remember?"

"I know, love, but… this isn't fair to you. You shouldn't have to deal with this."

Doug stared down at his love. There it was, naked as day. He'd wondered if, when the time came, if he could stay. And now he knew. He leaned down, kissing Paulie's cheek. "Til Death Do Us Part. We never got to say the words, but it doesn't mean any less to me. I'm here, Paulie, and I'm staying."

Paulie looked up at Doug's face, so dear to him. "I hope Taye and Marty are alright."

Doug laughed, crying at the same time. "Only you," he said, "could worry about someone else two minutes after being told he's about to die."

"Everyone dies," Paulie said, softly. "I just want to do it with a little dignity is all. And putting my affairs in order means knowing that all my family are well."

Doug kissed him again, on the lips this time. Paulie's lips were dry and chapped. Doug got him a glass of water. "That's why we all love you, Paulie."

Paulie drank deep, then smiled. "Ah. That's why. I wondered."

Dear Douglas,

I can't imagine how hard today was for you. In a way, I had the easy part today. I've been resigned to my passing for years. Ever since I came to terms with my illness, I've known that I've been living on borrowed time.

But you... you came into this relationship knowingly, but I think you actually felt that somehow I would be okay. But let's face it – even without me being sick, our ages made it likely you'd have to say goodbye to me eventually. It would've been good to have more time together, but we've had some good years together. Fourteen years as partners, husbands in all but the legal sense.

It's clear from seeing them during visits that, whatever problems Marty, Taye, Arthur, and John were having, they seem to have been resolved. That's important to me; I like thinking that my family will still be here, after I'm gone.

I'm having trouble finding the words to tell you what I want to. I know I don't have to say I love you. We've said it so many times to each other that it's almost instinct to say it now. But I mean it. I really mean it each and every time I say it. I love you, Doug. I feel incredibly blessed that we've had these years together, that you've grown so much as a person from the young man who stole his way into my heart – become a confident, loving man. If not for you, I wouldn't be someone's Dad. Not for real, the way you and Jason have made it real for me.

I'm so proud of Jason. What a wonderful way to channel his need to stand up for us! I hope that need to protect and help will stand him in good stead as life goes forward. I suspect the world he grows up in will be very different than the world we've shared, and I'm so glad for that. I hope young people like him keep leading the world into a bright new future, where young people feel safe being who they are.

I think the saddest thing is that I won't be there to see Jason grow up. To see the world that he and his generation will make. I bet it'll be beautiful.

For now, though, I need to put aside ideas of a long future, and focus on one day at a time. Because there are no guarantees. No way of knowing which day will be the last day. There's only the knowing that the last day will be here, soon.

I'm not scared. Not really.

Maybe a little, if I'm being honest.

I love you, Doug. I'm sorry you have to go through this now.

Love, Paulie

Chapter Twelve: Measure It in Love

Dear Douglas,
    I don't really feel up to writing very much today.
Love, Paulie

Winter 2003

Autumn kept on rolling through its course. It was unseasonably warm at the beginning of November, but by the middle, it felt like winter was starting to settle in. Everyone at 6 Kinsey Circle tried to stay busy in different ways to combat the somber atmosphere that seemed to have crept into the house that had been so lively.

Taye got his job back at *La Maison du Chanteur* and was hailed at Paradise Island like a returning hero. For several weeks, there were non-stop requests for him to sing pieces from *Ragtime*, and he regaled friends and strangers alike with stories from the tour.

Marty kept busy with his school work. He did Hanukkah shopping for his family, and for Taye, with whom it had now become a tradition. He did Christmas shopping for his friends, worked on a new D&D campaign, read his weekly comics, and did a lot of cooking for himself, Taye, and Doug.

Ken spent a lot of time with Michael, and the two of them began visiting Ken's gym together, much to the delight and amusement of Dave and Gus, Ken's old workout buddies, who enjoyed teasing Michael about what a jerk he was hooked up with, and telling Ken that Michael was too good for him.

Arthur and John spent most of their time joined at the hip. The relationship, which had been strained by the "wacky tobacky" incident (as they would later refer to it with a chuckle (but never when Marty or Taye were around) seemed to have been strengthened. They were often pulling out old boxes of photos, looking through them, and putting some aside for an undisclosed art project.

Jason threw himself headlong into the organization of his High School Gay-Straight Alliance, which they all jokingly referred to as the Rebel Alliance. He and Becky often worked together, and began to become quite close. They were often seen in the school library together, doing research for classes, or sitting together in one of the classrooms, working on posters announcing the Christmas dance their group was hosting.

Doug...

Doug found it difficult to stay busy, to keep his mind off of things, despite Paulie and Dr. Roberts' frequent insistence that he should do so. He went to work, left work, went to the hospital, visited until they insisted he should leave, and then went home and fell asleep. On Saturdays and Sundays, he was almost always at the hospital all day. He learned more about different forms of leukemia than he had ever known existed. None of them were good, but the one that haunted his dreams was like a terrible ghost, reaching out to chill the heart of his family.

One day, on a Saturday, he woke up to find that it was past noon. He sat up, with alarm. Visiting hours at the hospital had already begun! What would Paulie think? He had been up late, at the computer, trying to see what levels of legal recourse he had if Paulie... when Paulie...

He had fallen asleep in his clothes at the computer, then, when Jason woke him, he had stumbled to bed. Someone (Jason?) had removed his shoes, but he was otherwise still dressed. He tore off his clothes, wrapped the towel around his waist and charged to the bathroom, passing Jason, who was wearing an apron. He washed his hair and his body, trying to put his thoughts in order. Jason would be fine. He was busy with some project or another these days. He could always hang out with Marty and Taye during the day, if he got bored.

Doug stopped. Something incongruous wasn't quite gelling in his mind about Jason. Then it hit him.

Apron?

He climbed out of the shower as he finished, dried off, and wrapped the towel around his waist again. It was strange, but fatherhood had made him more modest. Sure enough, Jason was in the kitchen, wearing an apron. An inordinate amount of cooking utensils and bowls were dirty and piled in the sink. Jason had flour on his clothes, but he was smiling. He glanced at the sink, then back at his father. "Don't worry... I'm gonna clean up."

"What're you doing?" Doug wondered. "You don't cook."

"I'm making brownies," the boy said, proudly. "They're not as good as yours, but they're pretty good. Want one?"

Doug looked at the plate of brownies. He took one; it was still warm. He bit into it, immediately recognizing small flaws... not enough eggs, he thought, noting the slightly chunky texture. But they weren't bad, to be sure. "Why're you making brownies?" he wondered aloud.

"The Alliance," Jason said, simply. "Bake sale today."

"Today? That's today?" Doug looked at the calendar, wondered where all the days had gone that had happened in-between that terrible night at Dr. Roberts' office and tonight. He couldn't remember that many days going by. "I promised I'd help with that, kiddo," he said, softly. "Why didn't you wake me up?"

Jason shrugged. "You were so tired when I made you go to bed last night. And I figured you'd want to get right up and go see Paulie."

Doug felt terrible. Of course he wanted to go see Paulie. He wanted every minute he could with Paulie, because there was no telling what was going to be the last minute. But he couldn't abandon his son. His son needed him.

Didn't he?

"Jason, I…" he began, then stopped. He what? He wasn't sure what he'd been about to say.

"Dad, it's okay," Jason said with a lopsided smile. "The brownies aren't *that* bad, are they?"

"No, no. They're fine. But… I'm sorry."

"For what? Worrying about Paulie? Duh." He smiled a little. "You're supposed to be worried about Paulie. He's the other half of you. I get it. I totally get it."

Doug blinked. "You do?"

"Oh, yeah!" Jason nodded. "I didn't, when I first got here. Paulie seemed so… silly, at times. I think he was just trying to relate to me… badly. I don't think he knows too well how to be around dudes my age. But, he's sweet. And he's kind. And he loves you so much! So much that it made him love me. And…" Jason trailed off. "I love him, too. I'm just getting' to know him, but I love him. It was weird to feel like that at first, but now, he's just my other Dad. I get it."

Doug was stunned. He stared at his son a while. Then reached out, working out a flour smudge on his face with a thumb. "Next batch, add one more egg. I think you're using my old recipe."

Jason frowned. "I couldn't find your recipes. I looked one up on the internet."

"Okay, now that's just sacrilege," Doug grumbled. He went over and located the recipe box for desserts, which was on the shelf behind the powdered sugar, where it always was. "Here. Use the brownie recipe in here. And next time, wake me up."

Jason grinned. "Okay, Dad."

Doug ruffled the unkempt mop of hair on top of his son's head. "Listen, Jason, you know, if you really need me…"

"I know, Dad," his son interrupted. "But right now, Paulie needs you more, and you need him. So don't worry. I'm totally cool."

"You sure are," Doug said with a little smile. Then he headed to the hospital.

● ● ● ● ● ● ● ● ● ● ● ● ●

Dr. Roberts chuckled as he approached Paulie's room. He could already hear his favorite patient's voice, raised in some story or another. Then a nurse's laughter rose up over it. He entered to find Nurse Samuels laughing brightly, and Paulie smiling softly, his hands folded on top of his sheets. "Oh, Doctor," she said, startling to attention as the door swung to. "I was just in here to get Mr. Mayhew's blood pressure, and…"

"Don't worry, Nurse," Dr. Roberts said with a soft chuckle. "I've known Mr. Mayhew longer than most nurses have been in residence here. I know what he's like to deal with. He gets you laughing, and then you realize you'd forgotten he was a patient." He wagged a playful finger. "Paulie, you shouldn't tease my staff like this."

"Rest assured, my dear Doctor," Paulie said, with a wan smile "that I allowed the delightful Nurse Samuels to take all of my vital signs before any untoward jocularity."

"Jocularity," Dr. Roberts chortled. "Indeed." He turned and nodded. "That will be all, Nurse."

"Of course, Doctor," she said, excusing herself and heading out the door, still smiling.

"I should welcome you to the Paulie Mayhew Memorial Arboretum," Paulie said, sitting up a little with a wince. Indeed, the room was so full of flowers that it looked like a hothouse.

Dr. Roberts frowned. "That's not so funny, Paulie," he said. "You know what I've told you. Optimism is key to…"

"To what, Gene?" Paulie said, softly. Dr. Roberts was taken aback; Paulie almost never called him by his first name, although they'd known each other for years. "A speedy recovery? Any recovery at all?" There was no bitterness in Paulie's voice. Just a wry self-deprecation. "No, Gene. I have no optimism; only realism. And the reality isn't so bad, now is it? I'm fifty-six – a most respectable age. I've lived a good life, and I've lived for years after being diagnosed as HIV positive. I watched so many friends die when things got bad in the 80s, and I sometimes wondered why I lasted so long." He smiled, warmly. "That was optimism at work. This is just what it is."

Dr. Roberts sighed, sitting in a chair next to the bed. "You don't make this easy for me, Paulie," he said. "You're not just another patient to me, you know. You're like a friend."

Paulie reached out, patting the doctor's hand where it rested nearby. "I know, Gene. And you've been my friend in difficult times. But you can't help me this time. There's no miracle wonder drug... no new procedure. And it's okay. I've had more years than I might have, thanks to you." He smiled. "And I do thank you, Gene. Very much."

They sat there a moment. Dr. Roberts turned his hand over, taking Paulie's in it, and gave it a gentle squeeze, which was lightly returned. "I just wanted to ask, are you sure you don't want any priest or anything to come by?"

Paulie laughed a bit more earnestly. "Forgive all my sins at the last moment?" His eyes were bright with good humor. "I've never understood that. I could've lived the life of a serial killer, but if I get those Last Rites in, it's off to Heaven!" He chuckled and shook his head. "No, thank you. I've quite enjoyed my 'sins', and I don't repent them one bit. No, no. If my life has been sin, then I have no interest in Heaven."

Dr. Roberts chuckled. "Paulie, if there's any justice in the world, you're already considered a saint up in some great big, gay Heaven."

Paulie laid back, a smile playing on his lips. "Gay Heaven? Well, as it's long as it's not pink. So tacky. Also I think there's already a St. Paul out there, and he wouldn't be my biggest fan."

"Okay, okay, you win," Dr. Roberts said, putting up his hands in surrender. "Well, at least tell me you've got everything in order?"

"Oh, yes," Paulie assured him. "I had my will drawn up years ago, though I've made some recent changes to it. Most things go to Douglas, with a few exceptions. Odds and ends I want to make sure people get."

Dr. Roberts nodded. "Paulie, I want you to know, I've told all my staff to allow Doug to be here whenever he needs to be. No one's going to refuse to let him see you, ever."

Paulie chuckled. "Don't tell him. He'll set up camp here around the clock." Then he frowned, glancing at the clock. "Speaking of which, is it really 1:00 PM? And no Doug?" His frown deepened. "That's not like him. I hope everything's alright at home."

As if on cue, Doug came into view as an elevator door opened down the corridor. "Here he comes," the Doctor said. "I'll give you two your space."

He emerged into the corridor as Doug came huffing up to the room. "Everything alright, Douglas?"

Doug nodded. "Yes, thank you, Doc. Just overslept."

Dr. Roberts nodded. "Well, you've been burning the candle at both ends. You're not going to do Paulie any good if you make yourself sick."

"I know," Doug said, sounding contrite. "I think I'm starting to realize that. Thanks, Doc."

Doug went in, and Dr. Roberts closed the door. In his many years as a doctor, he had seen many couples go through this difficult time, and few had gone through it with the grace, the love, and the sorrow that Paulie and Doug were. He sighed, thinking how unfair it was, and went to see how things were with his other patients.

Inside the room, the two visited, making small-talk. Doug told Paulie about the brownies, and they both chuckled. "Jason's been saving up newspapers for you," Doug said, chuckling. "Every magazine and newspaper he could lay his hands on about the *Goodrich* case, for one thing. He says it's historic, and you're going to want to read them when you feel up to it."

"That's sweet of him," Paulie said with a smile. "I listened all about it on NPR, of course."

"Can you believe it?" Doug said with a grin. "Legal gay marriage, at least here in Massachusetts."

"I'll believe it when I see it," Paulie said, softly. They were both quiet, as they both realized how unlikely that was, given that marriage licenses weren't being issued until May of 2004.

"Paulie," Doug began. "You know… if it had happened any earlier…"

"Oh, hush, you," Paulie said, smiling. "We *are* married. I've never needed a slip of paper or a letter from the state to tell me that." He took his partner's hand, holding it, gently. "We've been together fourteen years, love. If we did get married, what would change?"

"Only legal things," Doug said with a little frown. "I just don't want… you know… as things progress…"

Paulie nodded. "Already taken care of, love. I had my lawyer draw up the papers years ago, and he'll deliver them to you if you need them. You have power of attorney, and you're the executor of my will." He closed his eyes, giving Doug's hand a little squeeze. "You didn't think I'd be turning a blind eye to what would be needed, did you?"

Doug smiled, shaking his head. "I guess I should've known better." He reached over, touching the older man's face, so dear to him. "You've spent the whole time we've been together taking care of everyone else."

"A pity I've been so dreadful taking care of myself," Paulie sighed. "If I hadn't…"

"Don't," Doug said, softly, interrupting him. "Don't bring that up now. There's no good saying 'If only.' Things happened, and we are where we are, and we just have to deal with that."

Paulie studied his lover's face a moment, and then smiled. "Who are you, and what have you done with my husband?" he chuckled, weakly.

Doug stuck his tongue out. "Hey, I'm trying to embrace your Zen-like acceptance of things. Don't ruin it."

"Sorry, love," Paulie chuckled, laying back. "I'm not really that calm," he said. "It's just that… well… I've had a lot of time to run through the stages of grief, you know? I keep thinking of something from an old Pogo comic strip. Porkypine says something to the effect of, 'You can't take life too seriously. It ain't no-how permanent.'" He chuckled, ruefully. "Existential wisdom in comic strip form."

Doug shook his head. "Your Southern drawl is awful. Why do Brits always sound like John Wayne when they try to sound American?"

Paulie closed his eyes and smiled. "Over-compensation, I expect."

● ● ● ● ● ● ● ● ● ● ● ● ●

Slowly but surely, autumn gave up the ghost, and the winter of 2003 settled in. The gray skies and occasional snow squalls made for a melancholy mood that punctuated the general feeling of waiting and concern that pervaded the house at 6 Kinsey Circle. Every time they visited Paulie, he seemed a little weaker. A little smaller. It was as if he had been larger-than-life, and now, he was slowly shrinking into the shadow of an average man.

Many people came to the hospital to see him. Casual friends. People he'd helped by giving donations to charities. People who mostly knew him peripherally, through others. The hospital staff were surprised to see how many people visited, people whose lives had been impacted in some way. Doug and the rest of Paulie's close friends weren't surprised. They knew how many people had been touched by Paulie's gentle generosity in some way or another.

● ● ● ● ● ● ● ● ● ● ● ● ●

"Tonight's the big night, yes?" Paulie asked Jason.

Jason nodded. He was already scrubbed up, with a fresh haircut, and Paulie knew he'd be going dressed in a neatly tailored suit he and Doug had ordered for him. "Yup. Still a couple weeks til Christmas, so we decided to call it a Winter Dance."

"I think that's fine," Paulie said, reclining against his pillows. "Some people may find it easier going to a Winter Dance sponsored by the Alliance than a Gay Prom."

"Well," Jason said, rubbing his chin, "we didn't wanna make people choose between proms. Like, 'Oh, I'm already goin' to th' normal prom. I'm not goin' to a gay one, too."

Paulie chuckled, eyes half-closed. Then he smiled. "And you're going with Becky Barbarino?"

Jason's grin crossed his face, slowly, almost shyly, like it was afraid to be noticed. "Yeah, I really like her, Paulie."

"I can tell," Paulie said, his smile's warmth lighting up his face in a way that hadn't been seen in recent days. "You rather glow when you talk about her."

"Do not," Jason said, his face flushing a bit.

They sat there, quietly, for a moment, then, finally, Paulie had to ask, "Jason, is there some reason you came to visit without your father today?"

Jason nodded, looking down at his hands. "I… I've been thinking a lot. You know, you really inspired me to form this Alliance, you and Dad. And I know it's all been the right thing to do." The boy looked down at his hands. "I just… now that the actual dance is here, I feel kind of weird."

"Oh?" Paulie opened his eyes, looking at Jason more carefully. Something was eating at him, clearly. "Why is that, do you think?"

"Well, it's just…" Jason shrugged. "Do you think anyone's gonna think it's weird that I'm there with a girl?

Paulie smiled, softly. "I would tend to think not. People don't think you're gay at school, do they?"

"No!" the boy said, quickly. Then, a bit more slowly, "Well, some butt-heads might say they think that, but I don't think anyone really does. " He looked up, into Paulie's eyes. "There's one of the guys in the group, and I think he kinda has a thing for me. Do you think that the gay kids at school are gonna think I'm rubbin' their faces in it, or somethin'?"

"In your straightness?" Paulie asked. "No, dear, I don't think so. Remember it's not a gay club; it's a gay-straight alliance. That means everyone's invited to the party."

Jason considered that, then nodded. "What if one of the gay kids asks me to dance?"

Paulie smiled, spreading his hands helplessly. "Dear boy, if anyone doesn't want to dance with you, they're blind. Just don't lead them on. Make sure they know where things stand."

Jason echoed Paulie's smile and nodded. "Okay, Paulie. I just felt weird talkin' to Dad about it. But I knew you'd know. You always know. I gotta catch the bus home so I can get ready."

"Get me a picture, dear. I want to see how you look all dressed up." Paulie's smile crinkled the corners of his eyes. "I know Becky is going to be dazzled by how handsome you are."

Jason ducked his head, red around the ears. Then he leaned in and gently kissed Paulie's cheek. "Love you... Dad."

Paulie reached up, touching Jason's arm, softly. "I love you, son. Go have fun."

As Jason left the room, Paulie's eyes closed. Tears leaked out from the corners of them, but a wide, warm smile was etched across his face.

• • • • • • • • • • • •

Ken was jogging in place in front of the stoop when Marty got home. "Forgot your keys?" the chubby young man said with a grin.

"I know, I know," Ken said, with an apologetic grin. "Normally, I'd ring up Paulie an' go through his place, but... y'know."

Marty's face fell. "I know. Well, come on in. You can scoot through our backdoor and get up that way."

"My hero," Ken said, batting his eyes. That got Marty smiling again.

As they entered the warmth of the apartment, Ken's jogging slowed and then stopped. "I hear you ran into Gus an' her girl th' other day."

"Yeah," Marty said with a smile. "Her girlfriend Lucy's really cute!"

"I know, right?" Ken said, with astonishment in his voice. "Before I met Lucy, I never figured Gus would go for the pretty, pretty princess type. You ran into them at the clinic?"

Marty nodded, sorting through the mail that Taye had left on the table. "Yeah, I've been meeting all kinds of people at the clinic. It seems like Paulie knew everyone in Boston!"

"I hear ya. The other day, I met people from his HIV support group. I didn't know he even went to a support group!" Ken shook his head. "It's like Paulie lived all these different lives."

"I don't think it's that," Marty said, thoughtfully. "I just think that he tried to reach out to so many people... to help anyone who needed it."

"He helped me," Ken said, softly. Marty nodded. He had no idea what had happened the weekend that Ken had found Paulie passed out on the floor, but he had been able to tell that something had happened between them. Something good. The very fact that Ken was back with Michael — something everyone in the house agreed was a good thing — seemed to have stemmed from whatever had happened between them.

"He helped all of us," Marty said, putting the pile of mail back on the table, barely looked at. "I feel like he was always there for me, when I was confused, or concerned. Even when I couldn't go talk to him, I'd wonder what he'd say to me, and sometimes, I could almost hear his voice."

"We'll have to make some What Would Paulie Do? stickers," Ken chuckled. "But, yeah, I know what you mean."

"What're we gonna do if… when… we lose him?" Marty asked. He felt suddenly small, and awful, sick to his stomach, as if the reality of it all came up and punched him in the stomach, suddenly.

Ken patted his shoulder, softly. "We're not th' ones who're losin' him, man. Doug's th' one losin' him."

"Poor Doug," Marty sighed. "I hope we can just… be there for him… when it happens."

"We will be," Ken said, and Marty heard something in the slender man's voice he hadn't heard before. Strength. Resolve. "We'll be there for Doug, always. Because it's what Paulie would've wanted. He made us a family, but we'll always be family for each other, now."

Marty frowned, thoughtfully. "He did, didn't he?" A strange thought was percolating in his head. "Ken… you don't supposed Paulie did this… built up our family so that Doug would have people around when he was gone?"

Ken blinked. Clearly this idea was new to him. "Probably not on purpose," he mused. "But who knows? Maybe subconsciously, he was makin' sure everythin' would be cool after he was gone. Makin' sure we were all there for each other."

Marty chuckled, then sighed. "That's so Paulie."

• • • • • • • • • • • • •

Becky Barbarino was a vision in red, which contrasted wonderfully with her dark hair. Jason's suit was black, but his cummerbund matched her colors. He'd intended his boutonnière and the corsage he'd brought her to be red carnations, but Paulie had insisted on white, and, somehow, that was lovelier and more dramatic. They made a handsome couple as they came into the room, and Becky was soon surrounded by admiring girlfriends.

Jason greeted friends both gay and straight who congratulated him on getting the whole dance off the ground, but he demurred, not wanting all the accolades himself. In truth, once he'd gotten things started, many other students had stepped up, and he'd almost taken a backseat, especially to some of the more outgoing students who now led the charge.

The music choices were popular pieces… Beyonce, Kid Rock, Justin Timberlake… with some classic pieces, like the Beatles, K. C. and the Sunshine Band, and the B-52s. Some pieces were clearly chosen for camp and comedy, but everyone seemed to love it. The gym floor shook to awkwardly dancing teens.

After a few dances with Becky, Jason begged off and sat to one side, smiling, surveying the dance. Everyone seemed to be having a good time.

A second glance made Jason reassess that idea. Off to one side, he saw Francis Ingersoll sitting alone. Jason liked Francis, but he didn't know him too well. He was one of the first people to join the alliance, but he mostly sat quietly at the meetings. He was very artistic, however. He had designed the group's logo, as well as a poster for the dance. And when he got engaged, he lit up and became quite animated.

The small, slight boy was dressed in a handsome suit, his hair kept neatly scruffy with an expertly applied bit of product. He was good-looking, and Jason knew from experience that, once you drew him out of his shell, he could be really fun to talk to. But no one seemed to be paying attention to him, possibly because not many people had ever brought Francis out of his shell.

Jason stood up, walked over, and flopped into the chair next to Francis. "Whew! Dancin' in a suit sucks," he laughed. "You takin 'a break?"

"Um… sure?" Francis said, looking around, as if to be sure Jason was talking with him. "Well, no. I haven't been dancing."

"You should!" Jason said. "It's a dance. Everyone's supposed to dance at a dance. That's why they call it a dance, you know."

Francis smiled, just a little. "Oh, that's why they call it that. I was just wondering."

Jason nudged him. "So, are you gonna come dance?"

The other boy shrugged. "I'm not really here with anyone. I just came, because, I figured, if we put an event like this, I should come. Because… you know?"

"Sure, I know," Jason said with a nod. "Like, we went through all the trouble of setting it up, we oughta go."

Francis nodded. "Well, it's different for you. You're here with Becky, right?"

Jason looked over to Becky. She was talking with her girlfriends. She noticed him looking and smiled, giving a little wave. He grinned and waved back. "Yup. She actually asked me to come." He felt a little funny feeling in the pit of his stomach when he said it.

"Lucky," Francis said with a little sigh. "I'm not really… you know. I don't have anyone right now."

"You will, though," Jason said, turning to regard the younger boy more fully. "Maybe not in school, but there's a lot of guys out there. You're smart, good-looking, funny, talented. You'll find someone for sure." He smiled, warmly. "If my… my other Dad were here, he'd tell you. He's gay, and he knows, like, a zillion other gay people, but when he and my Dad met, it was like WHAM!" He clapped his hands together for emphasis as he said it. "They knew it was them."

Francis' eyes were wide, then he smiled. "That's right; you have two Dads. That's cool. I didn't know anyone else who was gay until I joined the Alliance. It seems like the others are kind of cliquey, though."

"That happens to everyone, though," Jason said, with a shrug. "I know it'll happen to you."

"I hope so," Francis said, with a wry grin. "It'd be nice to have someone to dance with."

Jason heard the music switch over, and the Beatles performing "Twist and Shout" came on. "Why wait?" he asked, hopping to his feet. "Come dance with me."

Surprised was not the right word for the expression across Francis Ingersoll's face. His eyes became huge. "M-me? And *you*? Dance? But... you're not...?"

Jason shook his head. "I'm not gay," he said, "but I want you to come dance. C'mon!" He took the smaller boy's hand and pulled him up, still stammering. Becky looked over and her expression was confused for a moment, but then her smile broadened as she figured out what was going on. Jason pulled Francis to a knot of other guys, let go of his hand, and then began to twist to the rhythm. "C'mon!" he called over the music. "Paulie taught me how to twist! You move your feet like you're crushing out a cigarette, and you move your arms like you're drying your butt with a towel!"

"I know how to twist," Francis said, quickly beginning to dance, if only not to stand still on the dance floor. Other students around them picked up on the moves and hopped in. At some point. Jason became aware of Becky up next to him, and he turned slightly towards her. She was twisting wildly, her red dress flowing in abandon. She turned a bit more toward Francis, and he copied her enthusiasm. All around them, each time the Beatles sang a crescendo of "Ahhhh", people joined in, singing loudly, often off-key. No one minded.

When that song ended, "Love Shack" came on, and no one left the dance floor. Not even Francis. And now, more people were taking note of him, because his dance moves were infectious and enthusiastic. Soon, he was gyrating face to face with Sammy Taylor, and the two were grinning at each other. Jason turned more fully to Becky, who was smiling at him, singing along with the song.

Jason flushed, grinned. He felt warm and happy. He knew Francis would have a good time, now, and he didn't care if stories about him dancing with another boy made it back to anyone outside of the Alliance. If doing stuff like that was going to get people talking about him, then he intended to give people a lot to talk about.

• • • • • • • • • • • •

The call no one wanted came two days later. Dr. Roberts told Doug on the phone that Paulie's vitals were worsening. He was still very coherent, and he might last another few days, but there was no certainty. He suggested that Doug gather the people closest to Paulie to make sure that everyone had a chance to have one last really good conversation with him.

Doug was at work when the call came. He sat in his chair in his office, then stood up, walked out the door, and went to Kathy's office. "I... can we talk?"

Kathy looked at him. His expression told the whole story, and her heart went out to him. She might be his supervisor, but she was a friend, too. They had gotten to know each other over work projects and charity events. Doug had been there for her through a messy break-up, and she had supported him, getting him extra leave when he went to Maine to get his son. "Oh, honey... was that Paulie's doctor?"

"Yeah," Doug paused, trying to find the words. "He thinks... I need to..."

Kathy shook her head. "No explanations needed. We've got coverage. Just go."

Doug shook his head. "I don't feel good doing this. But..."

"Don't. Don't beat yourself up. We're not swamped, and, even if we were, we'd find a way to make do. This is family. Get out of here. Take as much time as you need."

Doug gave her a slight smile of thanks and left. He stopped by the house and broke the news to everyone. Phone calls were made, and, slowly, a pilgrimage to the hospital set out from several different points. When they arrived, Paulie was asleep. The group took up residence in a waiting room, quietly talking between themselves. There was a soft hush over them, as if they were afraid too loud a noise would wake Paulie up, even out here. The real dread, however, was that they had come too late. That Paulie would slip away quietly, before any of them had a chance to say good-bye. On some levels, Doug would've welcomed that. He didn't want to watch Paulie suffer, and a quiet passing would be a blessing.

Dr. Roberts came in and talked to them. Paulie was in some pain, he told them, but, overall, he was doing as well as could be expected. This was just sleep, he assured them; Paulie catnapped often, worn out by what was happening to his body. He fully expected Paulie to wake up within the hour.

No one left. Everyone kept quietly talking together until Dr. Roberts came in and told them Paulie was awake. He didn't advise them to all go in at once; instead, he suggested they go in smaller batches. Doug went in, along with Jason, to start. Quietly, after they left, the others agreed this was best. After all, with no surety of how long Paulie would be able to speak, it was agreed that Doug should have his chance first.

● ● ● ● ● ● ● ● ● ● ● ●

"Hey, love," Doug said, sitting down next to the bed, smiling. "How you feeling?"

"Oh, dear," Paulie said, looking at his expression. "I'm guessing Dr. Roberts called you in." He smiled a bit, touching Doug's arm. "I'm not too well, love. I've been… kind of passing out, now and then. I ache a bit… feel like I'm a bit dehydrated."

As he said that, Jason grabbed the plastic pitcher of ice water and poured him some. Paulie turned towards the sound. "Oh… Jason? Oh, thank you dear. I didn't realize you were there." He smiled, taking the water. "How was the dance? I haven't had a chance to ask."

"It was great," Jason said, smiling. "You were so right about the white flowers."

"White carnations for pure, innocent love," Paulie chuckled after wetting his lips from the cup. "No, don't blush, I'm not saying you're *in* love. But you like Becky a lot, don't you?"

"Uh huh," Jason admitted, blushing more. "I think she's awesome."

"Well, if she's smart, she'll think you're awesome, too," he said, half-closing his eyes. "Did you have any trouble with other lads at the dance?"

Doug chuckled. "He got Francis Ingersoll to dance with him."

Paulie's brow furrowed a little in confusion, holding out the now empty cup. "Who's Francis Ingersoll?"

"Well, um…" Jason poured more water. "He's the guy I mentioned. I think he likes me."

"Oh? You didn't lead him on, I hope?"

"No, no, I promise I didn't. I just wanted him to get out and dance and have a good time. He's really shy."

Paulie smiled. "That's sweet of you, dear. Shy people sometimes need just a little nudge. Ask Taye and Marty," he chuckled a little. Then his smile grew just a little serious, somehow. He took Jason's hand. "I know why Dr. Roberts called everyone here. I don't have too much longer to set everything in order."

"Paulie," Doug said, frowning, as Jason looked a bit alarmed. "There's not that many people here, and we don't know that it's super serious."

"Oh, please," Paulie chuckled. "I'm not an idiot, my dear ones. I can hear you all out there. I can hear the tone of voice you two are using, like I'm fragile. Besides, Dr. Roberts as much as admitted it, when I pushed him. You're all so dear to me, but we've only got so much time left, and I have things to say to everyone. So don't make this hard for me, alright?"

He reached out for Doug's hand and gave it a light squeeze. Doug wondered if he had any more strength left in those warm, loving hands. He'd always loved Paulie's long, clever fingers. "Doug," Paulie said, "I want you to stay, no matter else who comes in. There's nothing I can't say in front of you, and I want you to sort of... witness for me, alright, love?"

Doug nodded, sadly. "Of course, Paulie. Kathy sent me off. I'm not going anywhere. I'm staying until..." The sentence stopped. He couldn't finish it. He wasn't strong enough, still.

But Paulie could; Paulie could be strong enough for both of them. "Until," he agreed, softly, nodding. "Thank you, love."

Jason said, "Who do you want me to call in for you, Paulie?"

"Not so fast, young man," Paulie said, eyes twinkling. "I'm going to start with you. So sit, and listen to an old man ramble." As Jason sat down, Paulie looked him over. "Jason, you're a handsome young man... and I'm not just saying that because you look just like your father, and I'm legally obligated to say it." Doug chuckled, and Jason blushed, lightly.

"I feel like I want to offer you all kinds of advice for the future, but... " Paulie paused, thought for a moment, and then said, "But I can't. Your future is going to be another world from the one I grew up in. When I was born, the Beatles hadn't happened yet. No one had walked on the moon. There was no internet. And gay marriage certainly wasn't even an idea in anyone's head."

Paulie shifted in the bed, with a little wince. Doug moved to help him, but the older man shook his head, settling back. "I'm glad. I think the world is getting better in most ways. I hope so. The world I grew up in didn't have 9/11 either, or the JFK assassination, or the Bay of Pigs, or the Cold War."

He accepted the cup of water back from Jason, sipping it, slowly. "I suppose the best advice I have is to try and be good to people. I know how silly that must sound, but it's stood me in good stead for a long time now. I've just tried to treat people with kindness, because I believe most people are basically good when you really get to know them. Even the ones who show you contempt must have some redeeming qualities. If you can penetrate that barrier, they may be someone you want to know. Someone worth knowing." He reached out, brushing the lick of hair out of Jason's face, gently, then patted his cheek, lightly.

"And maybe those walls were only there because of ignorance, or fear, or because someone did something in the past that made them uncomfortable. I just think it's easier to win people over with kindness than political browbeating or by shouting louder than anyone else."

Paulie sighed, and then he smiled. "I know you'll be fine, Jason. It's not like I'm leaving you alone. You've got your father here, and the rest of the Kinsey boys. They've all got lessons to teach." He chuckled. "Sometimes it's what *not* to do, but you're a very smart young man. I know you'll be able to tell the difference."

Jason smiled a little. "Thanks, Paulie. I… I feel like I've learned a lot from you, since we've known each other. I just wish we had more time is all."

"Don't I know it," Paulie said, a sad little smile on his lips. "I want more time with you, with all of you. I'm positively greedy for it." His smile slowly vanished. "So I guess there's something I can teach you. Don't put things off. Embrace life. Carpe diem and all that. You never know how long you have in this life, so don't forget to tell the people you love how you feel about them. Say it often, and mean it. Prepare for the future, but live in the now."

"I will, Paulie. I promise." Jason came over and leaned down, kissing the older man's cheek. "Thank you for everything. For takin' me in. For bein' a second Dad to me. I do love you, Paulie. Dad."

Paulie smiled, his eyes bright and glittery with unshed tears. "I love you, too, son. Now, can you go send a couple of the other boys in?"

Jason nodded and headed out of the room, swiping at his eyes. Paulie watched him go, sadly, knowing this would be one of his biggest regrets – not seeing Jason grow up. "Speaking of the future," he said, looking over at Doug, "I changed my will a few months back. I set up a trust fund for Jason's college.

He'll be able to go anywhere he wants, for as long as he wants, and probably have a nice nest egg left over, I should think." He chuckled. "Trust funds are like food at a pot luck – better to have too much than not enough."

Doug smiled. "Thanks, love. I was putting some money aside, but..."

"I know. It's hard to plan that far in advance," Paulie said with a soft groan. "I understand that all too well."

Ken and Michael came in next, and Paulie's smile warmed up for them. "Ah, boys. Come in, come in."

"Hi, Paulie," Ken said, brightly. "What's the good word?" His cheerfulness seemed foreign in this room.

Michael glanced at Ken, then smiled at Paulie. "Hi, Paulie," he said, gently. "You doing okay?"

"Oh, no, dear. I'm dying. Didn't the doctor mention?" Paulie adjusted his glasses and winked. "Gallows humor, dear, I'm afraid. For some reason, it's the only kind that seems apropos at the moment."

Michael looked shocked a moment, then uncomfortable. He grinned, sheepishly. "I'm sorry, I'm not good at this."

"I should hope not," Paulie said, smiling. "In fact I wish not, for both of you. No one should get good at saying good-bye to people they care about. I'm certainly not any good at it at all. But, here we are. So I suppose I'd better get good at it."

Ken chuckled, sitting in a chair. "You? Pft. What do these doctors know? Knowing you, you'll be out showing half of them how to do their jobs in no time."

"I almost could," Paulie mused, softly. "I've been around medical procedures for years now. Maybe I should've gone for my medical degree late in life, eh? Certainly, I could give a few tips on good bedside manner." He shook his head, smiling. "Ah well. Roads not taken, eh?"

Ken leaned in. "Any time you want us to smuggle you out of here, Boss, you just say the word. We'll toss you in a laundry hamper and wheel you right out."

"Oh my," Paulie chuckled. "I did always love those prison escape movies. I suppose I like stories of people whose ingenuity allows them to do the impossible. Delicious escapism." Then he patted Ken's knee. "No, that's alright, dear.

If I really wanted out, I'm sure Dr. Roberts would oblige, but I'm comfortable enough here. I'm glad I stayed at home as long as I did, but, if I must be in a hospital, this clinic's rather nice. Food's decent."

Ken got a little serious. "Do you need anything, Paulie? Can we bring you anything?"

"Actually, yes," Paulie said, and Ken looked eager to please. Paulie gestured towards the plastic pitcher. "I seem to be out of ice water. Could you go to the nurse's station and get it filled? Mind you, if you go to the far station, they're next to the fridge, so there may actually be ice in my ice water."

"Understood," Ken said, with a chuckle, standing and taking the pitcher. "Be back in a sec."

"He will, too," Paulie said, watching the slender man half-jog out of the room. "Ever since I've known Ken, he's been moving. He was running away from something, and I didn't know what." He turned his eyes to Michael. "I don't know how much he told you about his past. I encouraged him to tell you something, at least."

Michael lowered his eyes. "I think… he's probably told me everything. I feel so bad for him." Then he looked up into Paulie's eyes. "But that's not why I got back together again with him. I really like Ken. When I understood… when he told me why he had trouble staying with one guy, I just… I wanted to give him another chance. Someone needed to step up and show him some trust."

Paulie's smile was warm and genuine. "I agree, dear, and I'm glad you were the one. Ken really cares about you. More than I've seen him care for anyone in all the time I've known him. You kind of slipped by his defenses, I think. And I'm happy he found someone like you."

Paulie reached out to give Michael's hand a light touch. "Michael, dear, Ken's a very special person. I probably don't have to tell you all this, but… well, he's funny, he's earnest, he's protective…" Paulie stopped to cough a few times, grabbing a tissue to cover his mouth with it.

"You don't have to give me a laundry list, Paulie," Michael said with a warm smile. "I know how good a guy Ken is. And I know he's fragile, even after all this time." The younger man rubbed the back of his neck. "I… I can't promise to be with Ken forever, but we're taking things slow, and we both seem to really dig each other. I guess we'll just have to wait and see. If things end between us, I'll sure try not to hurt him."

Paulie nodded, putting the tissues aside. "That's all I can really ask, dear."

"What did I miss?" Ken asked, coming back with the plastic pitcher fully restocked. He poured a cup for Paulie, then sat down, next to Michael.

"Just chit-chat, dear," Paulie said with a weak smile. "Hopefully the nurses didn't give you too hard a time?"

Ken rolled his eyes. "Like you don't know that you've got them all wrapped around your fingers. They can't jump fast enough for anything you need. They must've apologized fifty times for not keeping your pitcher full."

Paulie chuckled, softly. "They shouldn't bother so. Well, actually, let them bother. I find I'm enjoying being a little bit of a bother." His eyes twinkled with good-natured mischief. "Michael, will you excuse us, just one moment?"

"Oh, of course," Michael said, standing up. "I'll be out in the waiting room if you need me."

"My dear boy," Paulie said, smiling at Ken, when Michael was gone.

"Paulie," Ken said, with a slight squirm. "You don't have to say anything to me. We've known each other a while. I think we've always been close enough to say what we've felt."

Paulie shook his head. "Not everything, dear. Not everything." He sat up, and Doug helped push some pillows into place. "Ken, you need to know that… I've not always been proud of you or of your actions." The younger man's face fell. "Now, now… I said not always. And mostly, a lot of that was just worry for you." Paulie gave a smile. "In the last few months, I can say that I've been proud of you, each and every day. After what you've told me, everything you went through, I think you needed to tell someone to start healing, and I think you've already shown what a strong person you're becoming." He took both of Ken's hands, pulling the younger man down, kissing him, gently, on the forehead. "I'm proud of you, Ken. Very proud to have been your friend."

"Not just my friend," Ken reminded him softly. "Not just that." Paulie folded Ken into his arms, holding him there for a time. Then the younger man leaned back with a grin. "I'll try to always make you proud."

"I know you will," Paulie said.

Ken stood up. "I'll send some other folks in. You know if there's a restroom nearby?"

Paulie gestured across the room. "There's one there."

"Nah. Don't wanna stink up your private john. I'll find one."

Ken stepped into the hallway. "Next batch," he announced cheerfully. "Now, 'scuse me. I gotta do some business." He spotted a nearby restroom and stepped into it. Locking the door behind him, he sat down on the lid of the toilet. He sat there a moment, staring at nothing. His heart hurt so badly, he wished he could just die rather than keep feeling it. Paulie... the closest he'd ever had to a real father. What was he supposed to do without Paulie in his life? Emotion rushed in him like a storm, and he felt dizzy. As the tears boiled up, he buried his face in his hands and wept like a child.

• • • • • • • • • • • • •

"Hi, Paulie," Taye said, brightly, as he came in with Marty. Both of them looked a bit pale and a bit red-eyed, but both of their faces were smiling and cheerful.

"Hello, boys," Paulie said, reaching out to give each of them a very gentle hug. He had known for some weeks that, whatever had happened in the fall, it was behind them. That made him happy, because he hadn't seen what it was Doug had seen the night Taye returned, and he'd worried there might be something wrong. But no, it was clear that each was taking strength from the other, as loving a couple as they'd ever been.

Neither Marty nor Taye ever told the other, but, as he held them, each one felt how skinny Paulie had become as they hugged, how weak his arms were, and they embraced him gently, like he was made of old, fragile porcelain.

"What's been happening back home?" Paulie asked.

"Not much, honestly," Marty said.

Taye rolled his eyes. "Oh, except, you know, you finishing college."

Marty blinked. "Oh. Yeah. Well, there is that."

It was Paulie's turn to blink. "Wait... you finished?"

"Well, not technically," Marty explained. "But this semester is going to complete all my credits for my business major degree. I have to finish next semester to have enough credits to graduate, but it'll be kind of a coast. Or, well, it would be, but..." He grinned.

Taye elbowed him in the ribs. "Go on. Tell him how I'm a genius."

Marty chuckled, rubbing his side where Taye had poked him. "Oh, well, Taye's a genius, apparently."

"Oh, you're terrible!" Taye said, pouting. "I sat down and looked over the credits Marty had. You know how his parents had their hearts set on him finishing with a business degree?"

"But you wanted to go for computer science," Paulie said, smiling, nodding to the shyly grinning Marty. "You told me that the day we met. I know you've taken plenty of classes in computers since then."

"Well, Taye looked over my credits, and we realized I had enough to qualify for a double-major if I took all comp sci courses next year. I worked with my advisor, and he was able to help me find the classes that would get me the credits I still needed, so I'll be graduating with a degree in business *and* computer science."

"*And* what else?" Taye said, grinning.

Marty chuckled, shaking his head. "Well, Taye also took a portfolio of my programming work to a friend of his who works at a local software company called Maverick Three Studios."

"Who was very impressed," Taye added.

"And he's offered me a job, once I graduate. It's not incredibly well-paid or super-glamorous, but it's an entry-level job in the field I want." Marty grinned brightly. "So my folks get the degree they want, and I get the job I want."

Paulie chuckled, smiling at both of them. "Well, you two *have* been busy." He sipped some ice water, then he said, warmth in his voice, "I don't suppose I have to tell you two how immensely fond I am of both of you. Having you in the house... well, before Jason came along, I suppose it was your youth that was so infectious to me."

The older man reached out, tousling Marty's always unkempt hair. "You, dear fellow, have blossomed from the shy, awkward boy I first met into a more confident man. A man I've been proud to call a friend. I know your parents are going to be so proud of you, and everything you do in life. But I could not be any more proud if you were my own son."

Paulie turned slightly to more fully face Taye. "And you have always been as irrepressible a rogue as I could ever have wished to brighten my life with laughter." He chuckled. "And you have made me laugh. Oh yes. At times, when my heart was breaking, you've been there with some story, or some ridiculous piece of gossip, or just a gale of conversation." He laughed softly until it became a dry cough, which he sipped water to quell. "You may always need an audience, Taye, but it's been my pleasure to provide you with one over the last few years. I'll always be your biggest fan.

"Well..." He stopped, looking between the two of them. "No. I think I have to relinquish my claim to that title." Marty blushed slightly, lowering his gaze. "Don't do that," Paulie said, reaching out, tilting the young man's face back up to look into his eyes. "Don't be ashamed when you blush. You brought something so special back into my life. That sweet innocence. That wide-eyed sense that everything is new and wonderful again. How could I ever be cynical when I had someone like you around?" Paulie's grin touched his whole face, and his dark eyes were clear and bright as he spoke. "It's like I got to rediscover the world through you, and that's a gift I am profoundly grateful for, my dear Marty."

Marty's eyes were growing damp with unshed tears, and he swept his fingers over them to clear them. "Paulie, I... I owe you so much."

"Not at all, dear," Paulie said, smiling. "Not one thing."

"I do though," Marty said, more firmly. "I've learned a lot from you. Not just little life lessons about being a good person, but so much more. How to be strong. How to be brave. How to know what I really want in life, and how to be bold enough to go for it." Marty shook his head. "You're the most amazing person I've ever met, and I can't believe you've been my friend." As he spoke, his voice became increasingly choked with emotion. "Sorry. I'm sorry, Paulie," he sobbed, softly. "I didn't want to cry in front of you, but I can't help it. It's just so... unfair. There are so many awful people in the world. And so few good ones." Taye's face was sad and solemn as he reached out to rub Marty's back, softly.

"No, dear," Paulie said, offering the box of tissues. "I think there are just people. Sometimes those people are on our side, and sometimes, they're not. Sometimes we understand them, and sometimes they're utterly beyond our understanding. But I think anyone can be a good person under the right circumstances, and everyone deserves the chance to show it."

Marty turned to the side and blew his nose, and Taye shook his head. "See, Paulie, that's what Marty means. You're here, like this, and you're still teaching us." He dabbed at his own eyes with tissue. "You'll always be teaching us. Because no one can be as good as you are."

Paulie smiled, softly. "That's very sweet, dear. But I think each and every one of you is as good as I am. I'm no saint. I'm not infallible. I've been jealous and angry and petty. But at the end of the day, I just think it's up to everyone to decide what kind of world they want to leave behind them."

He folded his hand on top of the duvet and said, softly, "I hope, in my way, that I'm leaving the world just a little better than I found it. I hope that I've left things a little more loving, a little more kind…" His eyes flashed with mischief. "And maybe just a little more fabulous."

Marty laughed, even though he was still crying. "You have. If only by teaching me the difference between pink and peach. Peach always. Pink is just tacky."

"We were talking about repainting the living room peach," Taye said, softly.

"I like peach," Paulie said, smiling. "I wish I could see that."

In the corner, Doug, who was trying to keep himself contained and quiet, said, softly, "You will, love." This was so hard. He wanted to shove everyone out, to hoard Paulie to himself, but he also wanted Paulie to be able to say his goodbyes. He knew he couldn't be selfish with his husband's affection; Paulie had always had more than enough love for everyone in his life, and he had to try to be the same.

"Doug," Taye said, as if he'd just realized the other man was there. He crossed around to Doug's side of the bed and hugged him tightly. Marty came and did the same, and the three of them stood there a moment.

"If there's anything you need, at any time," Marty said.

"We'll be there," Taye agreed.

"I know you will," Doug said with a smile. "I'm lucky to have so much family."

Marty wondered again if Paulie had arranged things to make sure Doug wouldn't be alone. Part of him wanted to ask, but it seemed inappropriate, like asking a magician how his tricks were done. Either way, Doug would have family there to support him, so what did it matter if that family had been carefully constructed or came together by chance?

"Family," said Paulie softly, looking them over. "Yes. There are other Mayhews in England and Scotland, of course, possibly even some related to me by blood, but how is that family?" He took off his glasses and massaged the bridge of his nose. "Family should be more than just random strangers who share your bloodline. Family should be the people who mean the most to you.

"You are all my family," he continued. "In the ways that matter the most. You've been there for me at my worst, and my best. You've comforted me in my lows, and celebrated with me at the highs. The fact that we share no blood relation means absolutely nothing to me."

He smiled, reaching out to them, and the three of them came together with him to embrace. "I have been such a lucky man," he murmurs, laying his head on Marty's shoulder as the shorter man clutched him almost painfully tightly.

"We've been the lucky ones," Marty said, hoarsely, voice still quite thick with emotion. "There's no guarantee of having someone fantastic in your life. And you gave us a whole house full of fantastic people. I… if you hadn't taken me in, maybe I wouldn't have met Taye, and that… that would've sucked. I feel like I should thank you for that, every day."

"Very eloquent, dear," Paulie said with a chuckle, surprised to see the faintest flush of red on Taye's ears. "Why, my dear Mr. Dooley. Could it be that you, good sir, are blushing? Could it be that some of Mr. Martin's innocent ways are rubbing off of you."

"I am not," Taye insisted, rubbing at his cheeks, which were actually reddening more from the accusation. "It's too warm in here. You keep this room like a greenhouse."

"Well, I don't want the flowers to take chill," Paulie said, gesturing. "I mean, good lord, this isn't a hospital room. It's rainforest."

Marty laughed. "It is kind of a jungle in here."

"I'm just waiting for the tarantulas and macaws to move in," Doug said, dryly. "Then I'm out of here."

Paulie smiled at them all, and then looked at Marty and Taye, the easy way they stood together. "You two. You make such a good couple. If my bringing you into the home had anything to do with that, Marty, then it's I who should thank you." As Marty's expression turned to puzzlement, Paulie took both of their hands and put them together. "Young love is beautiful. To feel that I could've had even the slightest involvement in helping to create it is to make me feel like an angel." Then he chuckled. "But you're the angel, Taye."

"No, Paulie," Taye said softly. "You're the angel. You always were. I just got to play the part on stage." He leaned down, kissing Paulie's cheek. "Thank you. Thank you for the home. For the fun. For the love. For the good cooking and the games of *Monopoly*, and being a great rehearsal partner." He swiped at his eyes with the tissues again. "And thank you for Marty. We may have put the relationship together, but we couldn't even have started if you hadn't introduced us."

"I don't know," Paulie said, softly. "You two… some relationships seem to just be meant to happen. I think that, if I hadn't introduced you, you still would've found each other."

"Ugh. Way to take the magic out of the scene, Mr. Mayhew," Taye said, rolling his eyes. "I'm trying to say thank you here."

"Sorry, sorry," Paulie said, grinning, holding up his hands in surrender. "I should know better than to interrupt the performance."

Taye's face fell. "It's not a performance, Paulie. A performance would be pretending that my heart isn't breaking." He put his arms around Marty, who had begun to softly shake with sobs again. "I love you, Paulie. We both do."

"So much," Marty said, choking back the tears.

"I love you both, too," Paulie said, softly, smiling sadly.

● ● ● ● ● ● ● ● ● ● ● ●

When Marty came out weeping, the group held its collective breath. Taye emerged thereafter and nodded. "Arthur, John… you guys should go in and see him."

The relief of all of them was palpable as Arthur and John went in. Ken had rejoined the group, and no one had remarked on his reddened eyes when he returned from the restroom. He flagged down Dr. Roberts when the good doctor next crossed in front of the room. "Doc, how long do you think Paulie's going to be with us?"

The doctor regarded the group of them, their pale, hopeful faces, and he sighed. "I have to be honest — not long. He's very weak. He hasn't eaten for days. We've been giving him what we could intravenously, but..." He shook his head.

"But he said the food was decent," Michael said, frowning.

"Paulie's little joke, I'm afraid," Dr. Roberts said, a sad smile on his face. "Every time we change his I.V., he pretends he's tasting filet mignon, or sole meuniere, or lobster, or something. But, no... his body is shutting down, slowly. Frankly, I'm amazed he's still awake and talking, but you know Paulie. He's stubborn and very strong. He wants to say his goodbyes, and I think he's holding on until he does."

"Does Doug know?" Taye asked. Marty sat beside him, holding his hand, crying too hard to try and speak.

"Dr. Roberts nodded. "He knows. I told him when you all first arrived."

As the doctor walked away, the remaining Kinsey boys sat. As they sat quietly now, they became aware that this was now a vigil, and they were all determined to stay until it was done, to be there for Doug.

Ken realized something. Someone was missing. Quickly, he stood up and stepped away, dialing a phone number on his cell, hoping that he could get through in time.

• • • • • • • • • • • •

"Ah, I wondered when you two might pop in," Paulie said, grinning. His eyes were barely open, and his voice was quieter than it had been. Instead of drinking the water, he was taking the chips of ice and sucking on them, slowly. "I don't think I'm up for too many long visits, but..."

"It's okay, Paulie," Arthur said, sitting down. John perched on the arm of the chair, looking solemn.

"Good lord," Paulie said, looking between the two of them. "You two look terrible."

Arthur chuckled. "Gee, thanks, Paulie. We're only your oldest friends, sitting around, waiting..." He checked himself.

"Waiting til the end," Paulie said, softly. "It's alright, Arthur. I'm not deluding myself."

John's lip trembled. Paulie was surprised. He'd always thought of him as one of the strongest of the group. "John," he said, affectionately, getting a weak smile. "Oh, you stop it. Stop feeling sorry for me."

"I'm... I'm not sorry for you, Paulie," John managed to almost hiccup, trying to keep himself from crying. "I'm sorry for us. I know you're..."

"I'll be out of pain, soon," Paulie said, smiling. "No more worries, eh? Not so bad."

"Gee, you make it sound real tempting," John said, a little bitterly. "Scoot over in that bed. I'll join you."

"Now, now," Paulie chuckled. "This is Parting Glass stuff. I must rise, and you may not, and all that. Speaking of which, you know what I want, don't you? All three of you? Another wake, like back in the 80s, eh, lads? Except for real this time."

"Oh, yeah. Because that one ended so well," Arthur said, frowning.

"We were much younger and stupider then. All of us," Paulie said, softly. "But seriously. No funerals. No dull memorial services. If anyone cries on my grave, I swear I will come back and haunt you in an exceedingly catty fashion."

Arthur couldn't help but laugh, and even Doug and John cracked small smiles at that. "Alright, you old bastard," Arthur said. "A proper wake. Drinking. Happy stories. Music."

"Yes, I'd like that," Paulie said, laying back with a shallow smile. "Maybe I'll stick around until you have one."

"Well, that would sort of defeat the purpose," Arthur snorted.

Paulie smiled, regarding the big, burly man. "God, you've grown up so much. You were always the boy of the three of us. When did you get so bloody strong?"

"I had a great role-model," he said, softly, reaching out to take the cup out of Paulie's hand. It was getting dangerously close to spilling. "Anyone in particular you want at the wake."

Paulie considered then then nodded. "Everyone. Invite everyone."

John smiled. "You do that, and half of Boston will show up."

Arthur smiled. "It'll be a block party to end all block parties. The Allens will hate it."

Paulie smiled. "Actually, they sent flowers." He gestured towards a vase full of yellow flowers. Lillies of some kind.

"You mean Mrs. Allen sent flowers," Arthur said, eyeing them suspiciously.

"Maybe," Paulie said, softly. "Carter and I exchanged a few words across the street in the last few months before I came here. He actually wrote a rather nice note."

John shook his head. "Hard to believe, but I think you really could make friends with anyone. We should've deployed you to the Middle-East peace talks as America's secret weapon."

"I don't think I could've pulled off the accent," Paulie said, wryly. "And no one ever takes British people seriously. Too much Monty Python and Stephen Fry." Then he looked serious. "This is awful. You're two of the people I've known the longest in my life, but I just can't think of anything I want to say to you."

"We've had a good long time to say things to each other," Arthur said with a smile. "I don't think there's much left unsaid between us. Except good-bye."

"Ah, yes. There's that." He reached up and touched the younger man's bearded face. "Good-bye Arthur, dear. You're such a beautiful person. I'm glad you've finally started to see that in yourself."

"You helped me see who I was," Arthur said. "I forgot who I was when I went to New York, but when I came back... you've been an incredible influence on me. I've loved having you in my life, Paulie. And you," he said to Doug, who smiled, softly. "Thank you for helping me become friends with Doug, Paulie. I think we wasted a lot of years with guilt and anger, but the last few have been fantastic."

Paulie smiled as Arthur went over to hug Doug, giving him a moment with John. "Well, now," Paulie chuckled. "My first friend in Boston. And my first lover here, too."

"That was a lot of years and a lot of pounds ago," John said, forcing a smile, patting his slightly paunchy stomach.

"Oh, stop it," Paulie chuckled. "You're as handsome as ever. Who could ever resist those brown eyes." He smiled, reaching up to caress John's face, lightly.

John leaned over, kissing Paulie's cheek, and his face was crumbling into a mask of grief. "I can't say good-bye," John said, miserably. "Don't make me say it. Just say, 'See you later.'"

"See you later, Johnny," Paulie said, softly, eyes closed.

• • • • • • • • • • • • • •

Doug and Paulie sat together for a time, alone, after Arthur and John stepped out. Doug was fairly certain Paulie was asleep, and his lip trembled. Had he given up his chance to say good-bye? The door quietly opened, and he thought it might be Dr. Roberts come to check on his patient. To his surprised, he found himself looking into grief-stricken eyes behind a pair of glasses that had been out of style since the sixties. He smiled at once. "Mrs. Nussbaum," said, gently. "I'm glad you came. I'm sorry I didn't call to tell you."

"Hush you now, Mr. Douglas Pope," the tiny woman said, coming over to sit next to him. "Between friends like ourselves, apologies of this kind are not necessary, yes? Of course, yes."

She took his hand, felt how it was trembling, and gave it a strong squeeze. They sat together in silence, and then she nudged him with her shoulder. "I'll make you a nice pot of goulash when I get home. You and Jason need to eat, and it can't always be the McDonalds, yes?"

Douglas smiled. "No, Mrs. N., it cannot."

"Of course it cannot," she agreed. "Ach, the McDonalds. You've read this book, *Fast Food Nation*? Who can say what these so called French Fries are made of? Not potatoes, I'm thinking."

"Most likely not, Mrs. N.," came Paulie's voice from the bed, and both turned to look at him. His eyes were barely open, but he was smiling. "Thank you in advance for the goulash. I'm so sorry I can't have some myself."

"Paulie," she said, leaning forward, taking his hand in her other one. "This is so unfair. You're still so very young. A woman my age should not be at the bedside of someone so young like this."

"I know, Mrs. N.," Paulie said, weakly. "But I'm afraid it is what it is. My own foolish mistake led me here. And now there's nothing for it but to lie in the bed

I've made for myself." He looked at the hospital bed. "Metaphorically speaking, of course."

"Always with the jokes, Mr. Paulie Mayhew," she said, softly. "I should keep so good a sense of humor when my time comes." She squeezed his hand, but gently. "I won't keep you, but a little bird told me that, if I wanted to say my good-byes to you, I should come here and now. So here I am." She smiled at him. "You are a very lovely person, Paulie Mayhew, and the world is a little sadder for losing you." She leaned in and kissed his cheek, tenderly, as if she were tucking in one of her grandchildren for bed. "Shalom," she whispered, quietly.

Paulie smiled. "Shalom. Good-bye, Esther, you wonderful woman. Thank you for being my friend."

● ● ● ● ● ● ● ● ● ● ● ●

After Mrs. Nussbaum stepped out to join the others in the waiting room, Paulie sighed and turned to Doug. "Ah, my love. My dearest Doug."

"Paulie, just rest," Doug said, smiling. "You don't have to do this now. I'll be here, I promise."

"But I'm not sure I will be," Paulie said, softly but earnestly. "I'm not being morbid, love, but I don't know if I can stay much longer. Every time I sleep, it's a little harder to wake up. So I want to do this now." He took Doug's hand, gently, holding it with strength that Doug had not felt for a few days, almost a fierceness. "Doug, I can barely express everything I've felt for you."

"No, Paulie, please, let me go first, alright?" He laughed, almost a bitter sound. "If you start talking, I… I don't think I'll be able to get through all of the things I need you to hear."

Paulie frowned, but then he nodded, softly. "Alright, love."

Doug composed himself, then quietly said, "When I was younger, I didn't know if I really believed in God, or fate, or pre-determination. I still don't know if I believe in love at first sight, or if I think there's someone out there for everyone, no matter what Plato or Hedwig say." He chuckled, slightly. "God, this is hard. I've kind of rehearsed it in my head, but saying it is so hard."

"Take your time, love," Paulie said, quietly. "Take your time." Despite the comforting words, Doug thought that Paulie looked tired, almost exhausted, almost a ghost of the strong, vibrant man he'd been.

"I just want to say that… while I don't really know if I believe any of that, I do absolutely believe in true love. And I believe that it was no coincidence that led us to being together." Doug paused, gasped breath, choked back the tears, and continued. "I feel like you've always completed the other half of who I am. I feel like being with you has made me a better, stronger person. I feel like, together, we could do anything."

Then his face fell. "But… now…" He stopped, unable to continue. How could his last words to Paulie be words of doubt and fear? Paulie was facing the ultimate unknown with strength and dignity. How could he tell Paulie that he now questioned everything that had been between them, because he was going to have to go on alone.

Paulie seemed to understand perfectly. He smiled, reached out a hand, and touched Doug's face. "Don't, love. I know you're scared. So am I. I know I'm acting calm, but… I'm scared." He shuddered. "I don't know what comes next. I don't know if there's an afterlife. If there is, am I going to Heaven or Hell? I don't know." His face was so stricken, that, for a moment, Doug wanted to flee the room. But Paulie held his hand tighter. "But I have absolute faith in one thing: our love."

Paulie struggled to sit up a bit, and Doug helped him, propping him up with the pillows. "I loved you the moment you shook hands with me after that meeting," Paulie said with a soft smile. "I looked into your eyes — they've always been so bright and beautiful. And I was lost. Pushing you away, when you were still figuring everything out… that was the hardest moment of my life. I wondered if I'd ever see you again. But I had faith, and I was rewarded." His face clouded. "I've felt guilty at times. If it hadn't been for me, would you have married Linda, raised Jason, been happy in a different life?"

"No," Doug said miserably. "Linda would've been a mistake, because I would've always yearned for you. And I'd still be raising Jason alone." He slowly made himself smile. "Because of you, though, I don't have to do it alone."

Paulie smiled. Then he reached into the drawer next to the bed and pulled something out of it. One of his journals. Doug knew there was a box of them under the bed. He wasn't sure how many Paulie had filled since he started writing in them three years back. "I think it's safe to say," Paulie said, "that's it's now officially 'later'." He pressed the book into Doug's hand. "I didn't get much writing done in here, I'm afraid, and there wasn't much to say." He smiled, closing his eyes. "You can keep up the writing, if you want. There's still some space in that book, and a few blank ones. I bought a number of them once I filled the first one."

Doug put the journal aside, laying his head on Paulie's shoulder, softly. "I don't know, Paulie," he said, doubtfully. "It'd feel weird reading those with you not around."

"Don't be silly, my love," Paulie said, quietly. "That's why I wrote them. For when I wasn't around." He sighed. "I always wanted to say something famous as my last words. But I'm no Oscar Wilde, with his duel with his wallpaper… if those really were his last words." He sighed again. "Love… I don't want my last words to be remembered as 'My bed pan needs changing' or something, so I'm going to say some things, and then I'm going to stop talking for a bit, alright?"

Doug opened his mouth to protest, but then closed it again. Paulie asked for so little, how could he refuse this? He nodded, staying quiet, and listened.

Paulie looked out the window at his view of other windows, then turned back to look at the face of the man he loved. "I've made many mistakes in my life, beyond even the rather obvious one I'm dealing with just at the moment." He smiled, weakly, then continued. "I have not been a saint, no matter what anyone says now. Right now, everyone's remembering the good, but, at the wake, I hope a few of you will remember that I could also be rather wicked." He smiled a devious smile so playful that Doug couldn't help but smile in return.

Paulie looked out the window again, licked his lips to wet them, then continued. "I have, however, done one thing quite perfectly, I think… loving you was the absolutely perfect thing for me to do, and, believe me, you didn't always make it easy." He chuckled. "There were times, especially when you were feuding with Arthur, when I would've cheerfully strangled you, and I'm sure you can say the same of me."

"I'm sure there were times," Doug said, softly, "but, for the life of me, I can't think of even one."

"Well, that's kind of you," Paulie chuckled. "What I mean to say is, when I look back on my life, what I am most proud of is the people I've loved, and how I've been loved in return. I have tried to make my life be all about love. Love is all you need, as the Beatles said. Well, what did they know; they were bloody rich." He smiled.

Doug nodded, smiling back at him. "So many people love you, Paulie. So many."

"So I hear," he said, eyes shining. "But the one that has mattered most, always, was you. And that's what I want to think of as my last words." He pushed himself up, as Doug leaned in, and they shared a small, lovely kiss. "I love you, Doug. I will always love you. Always."

Doug watched the older man, his lover and husband of fourteen years, lay back on the pillows, close his eyes, fold his hands, and smile. Later, he would think that he had never seen Paulie so content as in that one moment.

• • • • • • • • • • • • •

The vigil wore on into the wee hours of the morning. No one wanted to leave, and several naps were taken in shifts. Dr. Roberts checked in one last time before he went home, and, when he came out, to the hopeful, upturned faces of those who were still awake, he could only shake his head sadly. Paulie was asleep, and Doug was sitting next to him, half-dozing himself.

Sometime about three in the morning, they were half-huddled together for warmth. No one had come to tell them they needed to go home and sleep. No one told them that visiting hours were over. And no one even thought about telling Doug that there was nothing he could do, and that he should think about getting some rest.

Ken and Marty were awake, talking quietly, when one of the nurses came hurrying along the corridor and into Paulie's room. Marty suddenly realized that there had been a backdrop sound, a soft regular beeping, that had changed to a steady sort of whine. He tensed in alarm as the nurse came out, hurried to her station, and paged a doctor. Slowly, those who had been asleep began to wake up, roused by the sudden tense change in the atmosphere of the sleepy hospital.

A doctor who wasn't Dr. Roberts came and entered Paulie's room, not hurrying, but looking grim. Two nurses came with him, and Taye, who was lined up with the door just so, could see Doug backed to one side, giving them room, his face pale. The vigil-keepers looked at each other, and a sad realization began to overtake them. They reached out for each other's hands. Some were trembling, and some were strong, but they all sat together, waiting for their vigil to come to an end, as it was clearly doing.

The doctor and nurses exited the room, closing the door behind them. The doctor caught sight of their faces and gave them a soft nod. "I'm just giving Mr. Pope a few moments alone with him," he said. They needed no more explanation. Slowly, the tension drained out of them. Marty turned, burying his face in Taye's chest, as Taye put his arms around him. Ken gripped Michael's hand so fiercely that it almost hurt, but Michael squeezed back. John laid his head on Arthur's shoulder, while Arthur simply looked down at the floor. Mrs. Nussbaum lifted her glasses, wiping at her eyes, and then reached out, taking Jason's hand, gently. He rubbed his thumb over her knuckles, feeling the wrinkled skin, feeling the tremble.

A few moments later, the door opened, and Doug walked out, shoulders drooped, eyes on the floor. He looked up and gave a slight, sad smile. "It was very quiet for him, at the end," he said, in a small voice.

As he stepped towards them, their arms opened, and he let himself stumble forward into the comfort and warmth of family, love, and shared sorrow.

Chapter Thirteen: Sunrise and Sundown

Winter 2003 to Spring 2004

Christmas passed with a previously unknown level of solemnity at the Kinsey Circle house. Lights were still put up, and gifts were exchanged, but some of the warmth had gone out of the rituals that had once been so cherished.

Shortly after Christmas, Doug went to see Paulie's lawyer and was told that he had been named executor of Paulie's estate. He wasn't entirely shocked to find himself the primary beneficiary of Paulie's estate, but he was completely staggered at the actual amount of money that Paulie's estate consisted of. Although he'd done Paulie's taxes for years, the money that had existed in the form of Paulie's inheritance from his family had long been held in an interest-bearing account. Doug knew it had to be sizeable because of the interest Paulie reported, but he was still unprepared for the sheer size of the figure in Paulie's bankbook. He returned to his accountancy firm out of the desire for something to do, rather than any actual need to make a living.

The Kinsey Circle house was his now, and he continued the ritual of accepting rent from its inhabitants, although it pretty much all went into a fund for maintaining the house itself and paying the real estate taxes. He also bestowed a number of items on them that Paulie had left them in his will.

Jason got the bankbook for his trust fund, and Doug couldn't have found the words to thank Paulie for the surety of the future that this meant for his son. There'd be no difficulty funding whatever college Jason ultimately decided to go to. Jason was also the recipient of Paulie's precious collection of Beatles albums, something the boy seemed to take as a sacred responsibility. They stayed where they'd always been in the part of the house that father and son shared, but now Jason took to dusting that area, carefully.

John and Arthur received shares that Paulie owned in a winery in the central part of the state. The news caused them both to blush a little, and Doug wondered if the spot held some special affection for them — some memory of love-making in the past. He hoped it did; he had learned to share Paulie with those who most cared for him.

Ken received a collection of vintage men's magazines, such as Colt, Drummer, and Mandate, that Paulie had purchased through the 70s and 80s. He had accepted the gift with puzzlement at first, but he'd soon found himself drawn, not so much to the art and photographs (though it was clear he enjoyed those, as well) as to the old advertisements. "Look how they posed," he said, in fascination. Everyone guessed that Ken would soon be trying some new positions in his modeling work.

Taye received a number of playbills of first-run Broadway shows in Boston, New York, San Francisco, London, and elsewhere. He also received a number of autographed photographs of performers. More importantly, he got a small black book with the names and phone numbers of a few important people that Paulie knew. He also got a small note from Paulie. "I never gave you these before, because I never thought you needed them. Your talent and personality are all you will ever need to be a star. But you might want to pass these over to your agent, just in case."

To Marty, Paulie had left a pair of curious airline tickets and a Visa gift card. "My graduation present to you," said the note. When he called the airline, he found that they were open-ended tickets to anywhere in Europe that the airline flew. The Visa card had a sizeable amount on it, enough to pay for hotels, meals, land transportation, and sightseeing for some time. "I'd told him I wanted to travel after college," he said, miserably. "But I'd wanted to, you know, write back to him, send postcards and stuff. Tell him what a great time we're having." The gift was much appreciated, but it was put aside for now. School lingered on, and Marty didn't know where he wanted to go.

The year turned and 2004 began. Although another snowstorm in January slowed the city down, Paulie's wake at Paradise Island was held with all proper lack of decorum. The owner, Joe, opened the place early for a select clientele that night, and a number of staff volunteered to serve drinks. Doug paid them large tips, although they'd tried to say they weren't there for the money, and arranged an open bar. Taye arranged catering from the restaurant.

Paulie's friends came together with the family he'd built to share stories about his life. Arthur and John had built collages using tons of pictures they had of Paulie, supplementing them with sketches Arthur had done and photos borrowed from other friends. These were set up on one of the tables, and people came over to look at them and sign a guest book. They dined on tasty French hors-d'oeuvres, told stories, talked, cried, laughed, and generally honored the life of the man they all had loved.

Afterwards, a smaller number of them stayed as the club opened, continuing the drinking, dancing together, and laughing more and crying less. Afterwards, Marty mentioned ice cream, and a small pilgrimage walked from Landsdowne Street to the T, took it to Harvard Square, and got Toscanini's, which had always been Paulie's favorite. Afterwards, they slowly said good-bye to one another, embraced, and then trickled away in small groups, until only the inhabitants of Six Kinsey Circle remained. They made their way home on the subway and by foot, content to largely walk in silence. So much had been said today, and no one felt the need to continue the conversation.

Back home, there were quiet embraces outside the house, and then each went to their own part of it, to ponder their own thoughts and feelings on the day.

The months tumbled on. February and March were fairly mild. Spring cleaning, put off in the cold weather, was set to with a vengeance. Many of Paulie's things stayed right where they were, like books, music, photos, and the like. Other things, like clothing, were taken out, looked over, and sorted. Some things were given to friends that they fit, some things past salvage were disposed of, but the rest was bagged up and donated to Good Will. Certain items were moved around, and a smaller bed was purchased, moved into the spot where Paulie's closets had been, because the spare room had never really been transformed into a bedroom the way it had been originally intended. Slowly, the top floor stopped being Paulie and Doug's, and became Doug and Jason's.

The small box of journals lay untouched on the desk under the circular window that Paulie had jokingly referred to as his writer's garret. Doug had taken the one from the clinic and added it to the rest, but he showed no signs of interest in reading them. In fact he showed little sign of interest in much of anything.

Doug bore everything now with a kind of stoicism. After his breakdown the night of Paulie's passing, he had handled all the rest of the situation with calm and a kind of weary resignation. It had been admirable at first, but now, his friends began to quietly worry for him. There was no outward acknowledgement of what had happened, and everyone was concerned that Doug was starting to bottle-up and drift apart from everyone, even Jason. To all appearances, he played a genial-enough host, a caring friend, or an indulgent father, but everyone felt that this was just on the surface. It was hard to know what was going on inside, and no one wanted to be the one to push Doug, to nudge him and make sure all was well.

● ● ● ● ● ● ● ● ● ● ● ●

In February, Ken asked everyone out to dinner to celebrate Michael's birthday. This came as something as a surprise to most of the group. None of them could ever remember celebrating the birthday of one of Ken's beaus since Joe. Maybe it was because they were rarely around long enough for a birthday to pop up.

Because Ken's finances were still not tip-top, Taye volunteered to get them a discount at *La Maison du Chanteur*, and they had an excellent time. Taye had the night off from work, and all the other waiters dropped by their table and did their performance pieces, much to Michael's delight.

Doug sat there, a bit listlessly. The others were concerned for him, but he smiled and was responsive enough when someone addressed him, but he didn't initiate anything. Somewhere in the middle of dinner, Taye realized something with horror. He sidled over when the others were a bit distracted. "Oh, Doug... I'm so sorry. I wasn't thinking."

"About what?" Doug asked, not looking at him.

Taye blinked. "Doug... don't you remember? You took Paulie here last year. For his birthday."

Doug furrowed his brow. Had he forgotten that? Of course. They had been here almost a year ago to celebrate Paulie's 55th birthday – his last birthday.

"Oh... about... yes. It's okay, Taye, really. I just..." He smiled, thinly. "Memories, you know?"

Taye smiled. "That was a good night. Remember? You hired the pianist, and we all stayed open a little later so the two of you could dance to that song from *La Cage aux Folles*."

"Did we do that?" Doug said, looking around, as if seeing where he was for the first time. "Oh… yeah. That was here, hasn't it? Good times."

"Yes," Taye said, looking at his friend with new concern. "Good times."

• • • • • • • • • • • • • •

"I'm really worried about Doug," Taye said to Marty back home as they were undressing for bed.

"He seemed really out of it," Marty admitted, pausing in just his undies to contemplate the evening.

"Teddy Bear," Taye said, biting his lip, "I think it's more than that. It's almost like he's in shock about what happened. He's fighting so hard to keep it together that he's just… out of it, completely. He didn't remember taking Paulie to the restaurant, and that was less than a year ago. Even after I reminded him, I'm not sure he really remembered it."

Marty frowned. "I'm sure he did. He's just got, you know, a lot on his mind. He's raising Jason alone now, and I'm sure losing Paulie's a lot worse on him than on any of us. I know that, if anything happened to you, I'd lose it, big time."

Taye smiled, softly. "I know, love. And same here. But let's not get all morbid now. I'm talking about Doug. He's not dead. He *needs* us."

"But what can we do?" Marty asked, spreading his hands. "We can't force him to grieve."

"I don't know," Taye said, miserably. "Maybe we need to have an intervention or something?"

"Taye," Marty said, taking his hands, "It's only been a couple of months. It's not like Jason is suffering. He's got all of us. He's eating okay, he's doing good in school…"

"Right, I'm not worried about Jason. I'm worried about Doug. This can't be good for him." Taye fretted a bit, then sighed. "Maybe you're right. Maybe I'm expecting him to just be back to being Doug too quickly. He needs to process in his own time." He nodded, then added after a moment. "If he's still like this in a month or two, *then* I'll worry."

• • • • • • • • • • • •

Things came to a head on Monday, March 3. Arthur came upstairs with some fresh bread and found Jason cooking pasta. "Hey, Arthur," the teen said with a smile. "S'up?"

"Hey, buddy," the big man said. "Wanted to talk to your Dad. He around?" Arthur was increasingly worried about Doug. About his withdrawal from the rest of them, his inability to express his grief over Paulie.

Jason's frown told Arthur that the boy sensed it, too. "Much as he ever is," Jason said softly, a hint of bitterness in his voice. "Dad's been kinda, y'know… out of it, lately."

"I know, kiddo," Arthur said. He looked over, saw Doug sitting on the sofa in the living room, tie undone but still around his neck, a beer sitting on the table in front of him, not even opened yet. It was like Doug was sleep-walking through life, going through the motions without actually experiencing what was happening, functioning on auto-pilot. Arthur came over. "Hey, Doug."

Doug looked up at him. A thin smile crossed his lips. "Oh… Arthur. Didn't even hear you come up. What's going on?"

"Brought you some bread. Just out of the oven," the big man said cheerfully.

"Aw, that's nice. Thanks, man. We'll have some with dinner tonight. We're having… um…" He looked over at Jason.

"Just spaghetti and meatballs," Jason said. "But bread goes good with that. You can mop up the sauce. I made the meatballs myself." The teen looked proud.

"Good job, bud," Doug said, a little absently. His face turned back towards the TV, but it was tuned to the news, with the sound off.

Arthur looked over to where Jason was cooking. What he saw made him frown. He grabbed Doug by the shirt collar and hauled him over to where the teen was working. "Are you serious? You're going to seriously stand here and tell me this is okay with you?"

Doug blinked in shock. Jason looked mortified. "W-what? Did I do something wrong?"

Arthur shook his head. "You're just a kid, Jason, I can't blame you, but…" Arthur pointed to the counter. "Spaghetti sauce from a jar, Doug? Shelf-stable parmesan cheese powder?" He shook his friend by the arms. "Doug, I once saw you rant for twenty minutes straight at the TV when the Urban Peasant said it was okay to use this crap. You're going to tell me you're okay with it now? Jesus Christ, man, snap out of this funk!"

Doug stood there, unable to quite get his head around what Arthur was saying. The big burly man walked to the refrigerator and opened it. "Look! You've got a beautiful piece of pecorino-romano in here, and you've let it get mold on it!" He opened the freezer. "And what's this? This is sauce you made with the tomatoes and basil from Paulie's garden! Remember? That batch was so good, you froze it for later. And now it's here, in your freezer, getting freezer-burned!"

He slammed the freezer shut. "Doug, buddy… we all miss Paulie. But you can't just fall apart and stop living life!" He picked up the cheese and shook it in Doug's face like it was like a faint maraca. "Do you think he would've wanted *this*?"

They all stood there, frozen for a moment. The tension in the room was almost palpable. And then, all of a sudden, Jason barked out a short, nervous laugh. That was all it took. The dam burst, and all three of them were suddenly laughing together, hearty, stomach-wrenching laughs that shook them down to the very core of their beings.

The laughter echoed through the old house. Sound had always traveled through the house's heating system with uncanny resonance. Two floors down, Marty and Taye heard the laughter, and they smiled, wondering what the joke had been.

Doug wiped tears of laughter away from his face. "Oh, my God, I almost wet myself… when you started yelling… about the sauce."

Jason was leaning on the counter, grinning. "Man, I thought you were serious, Arthur. That was crazy-cakes. I was like, this is some reality TV shit happening right here."

"Don't swear, Jason," Doug said, but he was still chuckling, grinning.

"Yeah, kid," said Arthur, with a grin. "Watch your fuckin' mouth."

Of course, after that, there was more laughter. So much so that Ken finally came up. "What the hell is going on up here?" He looked over. "Powdered cheese? Aw, Doug. Say it ain't so."

"It ain't so," Doug said, tossing the green cylinder into the trash. "Ken, what're you and Michael doing for dinner?"

"Well," Ken drawled, rubbing his chin, "Michael's out havin' a beer with some workmates, but I'm free."

"Good," Doug said with an emphatic nod. "We've got pasta for everyone right here. Canned sauce. No way around that, right now. But cheese..." He rubbed his chin, thoughtfully. "Ken, can you run around the corner for some decent cheese?"

"Yo," Ken said with a lop-sided grin and a salute. "I'll get that real hard stuff that Paulie liked. That stuff was always so dang good."

Doug nodded, smiling. "Jason, head down and make sure John, Marty, and Taye know they're invited to dinner."

"You got it, Dad."

When the two of them were gone, Doug turned to Arthur and gave him a huge hug that the bigger man returned with a deep chuckle. "I was half-serious when I started," he admitted. "I just... of all of us, you were always so proud of what went on a plate of food. Such a food snob. I just couldn't believe..."

"No, I'm glad you said it," Doug said with a grin. Then he sighed. He leaned back on the counter. "I just... I miss him so goddamned much, Arthur. He was... he was just everything to me. I feel like everything good in my life was tied to him. The house... all of you. Now I feel like I'm a kid playing dress-up while his Dad's out of the room. I don't know how to be a landlord... how to be Paulie."

Arthur grabbed the chair that normally sat in front of Paulie's writing desk, turned it around and sat, arms leaned over the back. "Doug, no one expects you to be Paulie. No one could be. We just want you to be able to live, y'know? Paulie... you made his life awesome, in ways none of the rest of us ever could. I know I couldn't live with myself if I just let you wither away up here."

Doug pushed himself up onto the counter, letting his feet dangle. He picked up the jar of spaghetti sauce, looked at the label and grimaced. "Well, maybe if I hit it with some spices before we toss the pasta in it..." He sighed, putting it

157

aside. "I know. I just… every night, I wake up at least once, and I reach out, and, when he's not there, it hits me all over again." He shook his head. "Some days, I'm just numb. And then it'll hit me so hard, I'll lock myself in the bathroom, turn on the shower, and just cry. Cry until my voice gives out."

"Well, it's only been a few months. You don't think you should be over Paulie or something, do you?" Arthur shook his head. "You guys were together for years. You're not just going to get over something like that overnight. Hell, don't you think I've cried over Paulie a few times now?" He shook his head.

"I don't really ever expect… to ever 'get over' Paulie," Doug admitted, softly. "But I know what you're saying. I need to plug back into life. Into 'us'. The 'us' Paulie made was — is — very special. I can't turn my back on that, even if I wanted to. And I don't. I want… I want this family to survive."

"I'm glad to hear you say it, bud," Arthur said with a smile. "We've been missing you pretty bad. And, hey, John and I thought of something we want to run by you. Dinner will be the perfect chance to do it." He stood up and whirled the chair back around, accidentally knocking a box off of the writing desk. "Whoops, sorry." He picked it up and blinked, realizing what was inside. "Oh, hey. Are these Paulie's journals?"

Doug nodded. "Yeah, I want to read 'em, but… I just don't think I'm quite ready for that."

Arthur nodded his understanding. "Well, once you've read them, unless there's some personal stuff in there you don't want me to see, I'd love to read them myself. I always wondered what he was writing in there. Diary entries? Poetry? Writing ideas? I saw him working on them so many times, but he was always kind of mysterious about them."

"Mysterious? He was freakin' paranoidly secretive about it." Doug chuckled. "You wouldn't believe how many times I tried to get him to show them to me." He looked at the box, then smiled. "Kind of ironic that now I don't *want* to read them."

"You should, though," Arthur said with a nod. "I bet there are some great stories in there."

"I'm sure there are," Doug agreed, "But it may be really, really hard to… hear Paulie's voice again that way. I'm afraid I might… really break down."

Arthur studied Doug's face. He seemed better – more himself than he had been. More awake. Maybe a good emotional release was just what he needed. "Well, you'll read them when you're ready," he agreed. No sense in pushing things. He had a feeling that what he wanted to propose at dinner would be a bit of a push anyhow.

• • • • • • • • • • • • •

It was the first time they'd had a big dinner at home since before Paulie's passing. If Doug wasn't exactly back to his old self, he was at least more with it, smiling more, more aware of what was happening around him. Arthur couldn't be sure he wouldn't go back to isolating himself, but it felt like perhaps a first step out of the shadows had taken place.

"So, John and I have been talking," Arthur said after they were all tucked in and eating. "We want to hold a party. Music, drinks, dancing — the works. We want to hold it after hours at Triangle Books, and we want to hold it this upcoming weekend."

"Not a lot of time to plan," Taye said, frowning a little. "Why this upcoming weekend?"

John and Arthur looked at each other, and then John leaned in. "Well, it's to celebrate two things. After years of negotiation, I've finally convinced the woman who owns the building the bookstore is in to sell the building to me."

"Wow, that's great!" Marty said. "You've been trying to buy the place as long as I've known you, John. What happened?"

"Well, I guess she wants to move to Florida and retire, honestly," he said with a shrug. "I can't imagine that she just finally saw the light. It's a big change for me. I'll be getting rent from some of the other businesses on the block, and the whole top floor of the building is a residence, so I'll be moving out of my apartment officially and moving in there."

No one said anything for a moment. They had all known that John and Arthur had often discussed giving up their two apartment arrangement and just moving in together at the Kinsey Circle house. No one was sure what this meant, but they looked at Arthur.

"Don't look at me," he said, smiling. "I'm not going anywhere. When we were talking about moving John in here, it was because it seemed silly that we were both paying rent. Now John'll be collecting rent from his tenants. It's a whole other ball of wax." Everyone relaxed, and John and Arthur exchanged a look. They had thought about moving in together over the store, but Arthur didn't feel the time was quite right for it. He wanted to know that everything was okay before he made any such decision.

"That's one," Taye said. "What's the other reason to celebrate?"

Arthur swallowed, then said, "Paulie's birthday's is Monday. We want to mark it with a big bash. In fact, we were talking about making it like a yearly party. We don't have to call it Paulie's Birthday Party or anything. Just take one day a year to remember a great friend and to honor all the other friends we've met over the years, the family we've put together."

Now everyone turned to look at Doug. Arthur bit his lip, looking at his friend. Would this help draw Doug out further, or would it cause him to slam the door shut again? Doug just kind of sat there a moment. Then he smiled. "I think that sounds wonderful. I almost wish we'd held off on the wake, now. You know how Paulie always loved those big to-do's on his birthday."

Taye laughed. "Oh my God, yes. Remember the year we hired the male belly dancer."

Marty pouted. "When was this? How did I miss a male belly dancer?"

Taye patted his arm. "Trust me, Teddy Bear, he was terrible. You didn't miss anything."

Ken snickered. "God… I dated that guy. It was the year before you moved in, bud. He was this college student who was convinced he was God's gift to homos. He had a great ass, though. You guys have to admit it."

No one admitted it, but they didn't deny it either. "He came in," said Arthur, framing the scene with his hands. "And he had those little finger-cymbal things, and he ching-cha-cha-chinged over and was like, 'Who's the birthday boy?' When he saw how old Paulie was, his face kind of fell. But then he brightened up and offered a lap dance. Doug almost punched him, I think he was hoping he'd found a sugar-daddy."

"Asshole," Doug snickered. "I really didn't see what you saw in him, Ken."

"I told you," Ken said with a shrug. "Great ass."

Michael poked him in the ribs. "So what happened?"

"Well, you know Paulie," Doug said, smiling. "He ended up making friends. He gave the kid the name of a dancing school he knew the instructors at, God knows how. Wrote him a letter of introduction." Doug chuckled, shaking his head. "He actually kissed Paulie on the cheek before he left. Maybe he wasn't that bad, now that I think of it." He sat back, smiling, thinking of Paulie. "God… so many crazy stories."

Michael sighed. "He was always really nice to me. I wish I'd known him better."

Doug smiled. "He liked you a lot."

Ken nudged Michael with his hip. "Paulie always had dubious taste. Terrible judge of character."

"Well, he put up with you, after all," Michael said with a smirk.

"Burned," murmured Jason to Marty, who chuckled, nodding.

"Well, if you're all cool with it, then we'll hold the party at Triangle on Saturday night," John said.

"I'm cool," Doug said, nodding slowly. "Potluck or catered?"

"I'm thinking potluck," John said. "I just dropped a chunk of change on the building, and I'll be paying for the booze."

"We can all chip in," Jason said. "We c'n make lots of lil snacky foods. Finger foods an'… stuff." He was trying not to swear.

Marty said, thoughtfully. "I do have a buffalo chicken dip that's pretty awesome…"

"I will *buy* chips and ice and soda," Taye said, firmly. "I don't cook."

Arthur looked at Doug and smiled. "You willing to make brownies?"

Doug paused, thoughtfully. Was he willing to make brownies? Brownies had been Paulie's favorite. He'd never wanted birthday cakes; he preferred a big batch of brownies. "Why do I feel like I'm being coaxed into some sort of occupational therapy?" he chuckled, softly. "Yeah, I'll make brownies. Wouldn't be Paulie's birthday without 'em."

Arthur nodded. "Just what I was thinking."

• • • • • • • • • • • • •

The party was a great success, and, although it was never officially spread around as Paulie's birthday party, with the day so close, it seemed like everyone wanted to raise a toast to him. People wished him a happy birthday in absentia, and they even sang Happy Birthday for him. Doug could almost imagine Paulie reveling in it. Although he pretended not to like people fussing over him, Paulie had always loved being the center of attention. Doug was sure he would've enjoyed this.

The next day, Jason had a babysitting job over at the Allen house, because Mrs. Nussbaum was out of town. Doug spent the day tinkering with the snow blower. It seemed unlikely there would be any more snow this year, but he'd always believed that being ready for the first snowfall of the following year was just as important.

As he crouched in the house's driveway, checking the fluids, he heard someone approaching and was surprised to see Carter Allen, apparently having just returned from whatever they'd needed a sitter for their kids during. "Uh… Mr. Pope."

Doug frowned. "Mr. Allen." They'd barely ever exchanged words. Although Carter had made it clear that he had no great affection for the Kinsey Six, he at least had been quiet in his disdain. There had been no intolerant language or threatening attitude. Mostly just contempt. Doug did realize, however, that the contempt seemed to be missing, which was something of a surprise. "Can I help you with something?" he asked curiously.

"Ah, I wanted to." He stopped, and then started again. "Jason should be home soon. My wife is just going to chat with him and pay him for his time." He frowned, looking thoughtful. "He's good with my boys. They really like him. He's a good kid."

Doug nodded. "Thank you. I wish I could say I had a lot of influence on that, but he's only lived here about a year and a half. His mother probably had more to do with it than I did."

"Mother, yes. I know he lost her a couple of years back. I'm sorry… for your loss."

"Well, as you say, it was a ways back," Doug said. "And Linda and I hadn't been terribly close, as you might've guessed."

"Oh... no." Carter looked down. "I meant... Mr. Mayhew. I'm... sorry."

Doug was truly surprised. Then he narrowed his eyes. "Mr. Allen..." he began.

"Uh... Carter, please," the other man said. Would surprises never end?

"Carter," he said. "I just... this is kind of... I've always gathered that you weren't exactly *fond* of us. Of Paulie."

No, I guess I've done a pretty good job of making that clear over the years," Allen said, frowning. "Would you be surprised to learn that... I'm sorry for that?"

Doug folded his arms. "Well, I don't know. A little. This just seems like it's coming out of nowhere."

"Not nowhere," Carter said, thoughtfully. "A... some months back, I sent a thank you through Jason. I don't know if you understood at the time, but Josie had just... and I mean *just* told me about you and... Paulie. About how you helped us when my back was injured."

"Paulie thought that was what you'd meant," Doug said, dubiously. "So, okay. You're welcome."

Carter finally sighed. "Look, I'm sorry. You're not making this easy, and maybe I don't deserve it to be easy, but I really do want to say... that I'm sorry about Paulie. I'm sorry for your loss... and I'm sorry I never got to know him." He fidgeted with his hands, pulling off his glove, flexing his fingers. "I'm not really very good with admitting that I'm wrong about things. But I feel like... I wasted the chance to have a friend."

Doug nodded, slowly. This was familiar, suddenly, and he realized he'd had a similar conversation with Arthur a couple of years previous. "Well, I'm sorry you missed your chance with Paulie, but we can always kind of start over, if that's what you're asking for." He extended his hand. "Douglas Pope."

Carter regarding the hand a moment, then smiled a little, putting his own bare hand out to shake. "Carter Allen."

The two men shook hands, and Doug asked, "Did you want to come up, have a cup of coffee? We've got one of those Keurig things with the cups. Paulie saw one at my office when he was visiting a year or so back, and he just had to have one."

Carter looked over his shoulder at his own house. "I should get in. Wanted to spend some time with the boys. Charlie's having a little trouble with math, and I promised I'd help him with his homework." He grimaced. "Math is not my strong suit, but…"

Doug arched an eyebrow. "I… well… I don't want to be too forward, but I *am* an accountant. Math is kind of my thing. Would you like me to… ?"

Carter raised his own eyebrows. "You… yeah, I guess I'd heard that somewhere." He looked at his house again, then back. "If you're offering, I'm not gonna turn down professional help. You want to come over, say hi? I don't have a fancy coffee machine, but we do okay."

"Sure," Doug said. He looked down at the snow-blower. It could wait. Paulie would've been the first to say that people mattered more than things, and there wouldn't be any more snow this year, he suspected. "Let me just wash up. Oh, and we've got some brownies leftover. I'll bring them along."

"Love brownies," Carter said with a nod. "Okay, see you over there."

Doug watched him go. He went inside, washed up, grabbed one of the leftover trays of brownies from Paulie's party. Somehow, the desire to have too much food over too little had gotten out of control, and they'd made enough brownies to feed armies. Jason's baking skills were already noticeably improving; he felt a little proud about that.

He stopped as he crossed Paulie's "garret". He looked at the various items sitting on Paulie's desk. A pen and pencil set he'd bought for Paulie as a bit of a tease when he said he intended to start writing more. An old word processor – Doug wasn't even sure if it worked any more, or if Paulie'd ever used it. It had been here when he'd moved in, and he'd never seen Paulie so much as touch it. A string of four photographs of the two of them, together. He remembered that, taken at one of the cheesy booths at Hampton Beach. He was behind Paulie, arms around his neck, the older man caught in mid-laugh. Paulie's laugh had always brightened things around him. It was infectious.

"I don't know how you pulled this one off, Paulie," he chuckled. "Bringing brownies to Carter Allen's house. But good job."

He went downstairs and crossed the street into the unknown.

• • • • • • • • • • • • •

The end of March brought weather that was positively hot. Without Paulie there to tend it, the yard at Kinsey Six quickly became unkempt at best. One weekend, Doug decided that enough was enough. He and Jason headed to the local Home Depot, purchased mulch and a bunch of pairs of work gloves (since they always seemed to disappear), and came home and started to work. Although they didn't ask anyone for help, one by one, the various inhabitants of the house came out and pitched in. Flagstones were pulled up, weeds were removed, edges were trimmed. Even Taye, who reminded everyone how much he despised yard work, came out and helped do some raking. When all was said and done, the yard looked bare, but orderly. With Doug's permission, Marty pegged off an area to plant herbs, and Jason went to the bare part of the yard where nothing grew and scattered a bag of wildflower seeds over it. In what seemed only days, the bare patch of yard was getting green. By the time April came along, little sprays of white and yellow flowers were peeking out. By May, there were colorful blooms of red, purple, blue, and orange joining them.

Paulie's journals remained untouched, sitting on the desk where so many of them had been written. Doug would glance at the box, now and then, and remind himself that he needed to look at the journals, that he owed it to Paulie. But, somehow, now that he was feeling more emotionally ready to consider them, there was always something going on. He knew the right day would present itself.

And eventually it did. Jason was out of the house at an Easter-themed Bunny Hop that his Alliance had planned. Doug had said hello to Becky as she'd swung by, complimented her on her outfit, which was adorable, and sent them both off. Arthur and John were often staying at the apartment over the bookstore these days. Marty and Taye were visiting the Millers. Ken and Michael were headed out to the movies. They'd invited Doug along, but he'd declined, because he wanted to get some food ready for the week. Without Paulie around, Doug had found that he could sort of put together the elements of meals, then rely on Jason to finish them off before he got home from work. They made a pretty good team, he had to admit.

After chopping vegetables, measuring out spices, and making sure they were packed together in zip-loc bags with a set of printed instructions, Doug looked at the clock. It was still early. Earlier than he'd thought he'd finish.

He slipped a cup into the coffee-maker, set his mug in place, and sat down, watching it work. What would he do with his time? His gaze wandered around the room, lingering on various objects, mentally checking-off a list of things he should be doing. He slowly realized that he had handled most of the projects he'd intended to tackle.

Except one very important one.

He sighed, looking at the box on the desk. It wasn't that he was putting off reading them any more… or was he? He frowned, thinking about it. Was he deliberately avoiding reading them? He had never been the sort of person who had avoided responsibility, or kept away from difficult situations. But he had to face the truth, now… he was afraid of what emotions might be dredged up by reading the journals.

He stood up, walked over to the writing desk. He opened the box, and then pulled one out. He cracked the cover and read the dates, then closed it, immediately. That was the last journal; the one from the hospital. He didn't want to start with that one. He sat down at the desk, emptying the box out, then putting it aside. There were a number of journals that all looked the same, and one that was a different colored cover. He picked that one up. Paulie had said that he'd bought a bunch of identical ones after he filled the first one, so this book must be the first.

Doug opened it, and smiled, seeing Paulie's familiar handwriting set in neat rows. He flipped to the beginning. The first part of it seemed to be mostly a writing journal. Paulie had written some story ideas, a few fragments of stories, some of his poetry. Doug scanned through it, wondering if he'd picked up the right book. About a quarter of the way through, there were two pages torn out. He found the two torn and folded up pages stuck a few pages later. They looked like they'd been crumpled up, but not discarded. He unfolded them, smoothed them out, and chuckled, seeing Paulie's abortive attempts to begin a journal. "Call me Ishmael," he snickered. Then he sighed, seeing how he'd finally started.

Dear Douglas,

Doug stopped reading, traced the lines of his own name with a fingertip. "Paulie," he said, softly, to himself. Then he opened and began to read again.

He read through the first few entries, smiling as he read Paulie's descriptions of spring at the house. A lot of the entries ended in amusing ways, with Paulie saying that Doug had just passed him en route to the shower and was about to get company, or that Doug was feeling frisky. The entries mentioned Martin Miller coming by to look at the apartment, and the way the young man had fit right in with the rest of them. Through the entries made over the first day, he saw Taye's crush on Marty begin, saw his own feud with Arthur for the ugliness it was, saw Paulie's worries for Ken. He realized how much Paulie cared about Ken, how worried he always was.

And in many lines, his raw love and concern for Doug was evident. Paulie knew that, no matter what happened, there would come a day when the two of them would be parted. Paulie had dreaded that day, not for his own mortality, but for how it would affect Doug. Doug felt a sharp sense of distress. Paulie was a giving person; he'd known that from before anything romantic had passed between them. To know now that much of the worry Paulie had had in the last few years was because of him...

Doug closed the journal a moment, and closed his eyes, feeling his heart ache. Paulie shouldn't have needed to worry so much. Then he opened both again, reading on. The other thing that the journal made clear was how deeply and truly Paulie loved him. And how completely Paulie felt loved in return. That made it easier to bear, to know that Paulie knew how much and how deeply Doug had cared for him.

Doug got to what seemed to be a logical point to pause and got up to grab his long-forgotten coffee. He drank, feeling like he'd been reading for hours, when it had only really been an hour or so. And then he looked at the next entry. The date... had everything he'd read so far only been a few days? Paulie's journal-keeping had been intensely methodical, keeping note, not only of events, but of conversations, emotions, hear-say, and more writing notes, ideas, fragments, poems. Doug felt his heart swell. This wasn't just a journal; this was like having Paulie around to tell him stories about everything that'd happened on the days he had written about. He could hear his lover's voice in the journal entries, and it made him smile and feel... like he wasn't alone.

● ● ● ● ● ● ● ● ● ● ● ●

"I'm telling you, Arthur," Doug said over dinner that night, "they're incredible!"

"They sound incredible," Arthur agreed. He'd come over to have an early dinner with Doug, so it was just the two of them, alone. "I told you they were going to be awesome to have."

Doug was smiling as he passed over the platter of steaks. It had been warm enough that it hadn't seemed strange to hit the butcher's for some steak and then break out the grill. Oven-roasted potatoes, a light salad, and, yes, some fresh-baked bread rounded out the meal. "Well, fine, you were right, then. Paulie wrote down conversations, impressions, even speculation on what was happening when we weren't all together. He left some things out, like he talks about talking with Ken last year, but he doesn't mention exactly what Ken said, just that he felt he understood a lot better where Ken was coming from, and that he hoped Ken had gotten out a lot of things that had been unsaid for a long time."

"Well," Arthur said as he poured himself another glass of the wine he'd brought over, "you have to figure Paulie knew you'd read these someday. He probably didn't want to betray Ken's trust."

"Ken's really... well... grown-up doesn't seem like the right term, does it?" Doug rubbed his chin. "Matured? I don't know."

"He's changed a lot over the last year," Arthur said with a nod at Doug's empty wineglass. "And I'd say, over all, it's for the better."

Doug nodded, offering his glass for a refill as well. "I'd say so. I don't think he's... well, whatever it was that was bothering him isn't gone, but it's like it's been put to rest. I think he needed to tell someone something, and that someone ended up being Paulie." He watched Arthur pour the red wine, then added thoughtfully, "Whatever it was, I know Paulie was more tender to him after their talk, and Ken just seems more together. Anyway, it's a good change, like you said."

"Yeah, change," said Arthur, and Doug immediately heard the note of nervousness in his voice. "I... wanted to talk to you about something — a possible change."

"Oh?" Doug swirled the wine in the glass, aerating it, gently. "Why do I think I'm not going to like this?"

Arthur sighed. "Listen, Doug, John… he's asked me… if I'd like to move in with him. Over Triangle Books, I mean." He bit his lip. "It would mean a little more money in my pocket, but that's not really the point."

"You want to be with him, don't you?" Doug said, smiling a little. "Then you should be."

"But, it's not just that," Arthur said, frowning. "It's… John and I… we've been through a lot together, over the years. But I feel like… our relationship has always kind of been touched by Paulie's shadow."

The big man set his glass down, looked into Doug's eyes. "When John and I first met, when we hooked up back in the day, he was already living with Paulie. So when I came in, I was like a third partner. They never made me feel like it, but I was always kind of aware of that fact, in the back of my mind." He sighed, looking down at his plate. "Then I freaked out and ran away from both of them. And when I came back, well, apparently John thought I was hooked back up with Paulie because Paulie gave me a room in the house. We cleared the air when we started seeing each other again, but, even after that, I was still living down in the basement, kind of… doing penance, if you will."

He looked back up, into Doug's eyes. "Paulie forgave me. You forgave me. But what happened to Paulie… I've never completely forgiven myself."

Doug felt his heart go out to his big friend. "Hey, Arthur. Don't do this to yourself, man."

"No, no, it's okay." He smiled a little bit. "At Paulie's birthday party… I never told you this…" He picked up his glass, took a little sip, then leaned back. "I had, I don't know, a feeling? I can't call it a vision, 'cause I didn't see anything. But as we were telling stories about Paulie, and laughing, and drinking. I had the funniest feeling… like Paulie was there, with us, listening and laughing along."

The thought of it made Doug's heart ache a little, but it made him smile, too, eyes a little damp. "I know he was."

"No, I mean like he *really* was there!" insisted Arthur, eyes widening. "The feeling was so strong, I kind of stopped remembering to be all cynical and agnostic for a few minutes. Like… I could believe in ghosts, or angels. And… I felt… forgiven. Like really forgiven. Blessed, almost." He smiled, eyes crinkling at the corners in a way that almost made Doug think of Paulie. "I've been at peace about what happened since then, but I wanted to stay, until I knew you were okay."

Doug looked at Arthur's face. Not all that long ago, Arthur moving out would've made him happy. Now, the idea hurt deep inside.

Arthur saw the smaller man's expression, and immediately smiled. "But, if it'll be tough, money-wise…"

"Oh, no. That's not it at all," Doug chuckled. "Remember how we used to tease Paulie and say that he was the idle rich? Um… well… he kind of was. Rich, I mean. And now… I guess I am."

"Seriously?" Arthur said, a bit surprised. "I mean, I knew Paulie was well-off, but…"

"You wouldn't believe it. Hell, I wouldn't have believed it if I hadn't seen the bankbook. But I think Paulie was content to live as we did, and certainly we never wanted for anything. But, yeah, if I'd needed to buy an extra limo or two, Paulie could've signed that check and had plenty to spare."

"Wow," Arthur said, blinking at the thought. "Well, still, I don't want to think I'm leaving you in the lurch."

"Oh, Arthur, you're not," Doug said, getting up and coming around the table to hug him. "You're still family. John living above Triangle Books hasn't stopped him from half-living here with you these last couple of months. It's only a few T stops away."

Arthur nodded, hugging back fiercely. "It's just… I need to try and have a life with John. This house has got so many wonderful memories for me. But it'll always be Paulie's house to John and I."

"I know just what you mean," Doug said, smiling ruefully. "It's just a little sad. It's like an ending."

"No way," Arthur said with a grin. "It's a beginning."

● ● ● ● ● ● ● ● ● ● ● ●

Marty and Taye were deeply entrenched in their plans to go to Europe when Arthur and Doug held a house meeting to tell everyone of the impending move. The feeling in the house was universal. Everyone was a little sad, but everyone understood. It was the logical next step for Arthur and John, a chance to deepen the relationship they'd rekindled.

"The timing just kind of sucks," Taye said, sadly. "We're looking at flying to Paris two days after you plan to move. The house'll be half empty." He looked at Doug. "You going to be okay with that?"

"I'll be fine," Doug said, smiling. "Arthur and John are just going to be a mile or two away. It's not like they're headed to… where is it now?"

"Paris, first," Taye said, excitedly. "Then Bruges. Then Amsterdam. Oh, you'll love Amsterdam, Teddy Bear! They have the best Indonesian food!"

"Oh, good," Marty said with a raised eyebrow. "I'm tired of all this crappy Indonesian food we've been eating."

"You have no idea! You can't get it in Boston!" Taye exclaimed, waving his arms in frustration. "It's so good. Anyway, you can get it in the Netherlands. Then we're going to Germany, to sail down the Rhine and the Danube before heading down through the Swiss Alps by train into Italy. And then Venice, Florence, Rome." He sighed. "Quel romantique!"

"Indeed," Doug said with a chuckle. He didn't know how much money Paulie had left Marty for the trip, but he had a feeling it was sizeable. "Well, it'll be easier for me to find Arthur than it will be to talk to you two for a while."

"I'm sorry, Doug," Marty said, frowning. "The only way I could get this trip in was to do it right after graduation, because Maverick Three wants me to start in July."

"Hey, don't be sorry. Europe's awesome. And it's not like you knew Arthur's move-out coincided with your trip." He looked over at Jason. "Been a long time since I've done any traveling myself. Jason, you wanna go anywhere this summer?"

Jason shrugged. "If you want, Dad, sure." Doug chuckled inwardly, knowing that any reticence to travel was most likely because of a deepening relationship between his son and Becky Barbarino. Indeed, they were out quite a lot lately. He knew, however, that, thanks to Paulie, he'd likely never have to remind his son to have safe sex.

"Maybe we'll do some camping. I used to go camping a lot when I was a kid. Want to do some weekend trips?" Doug grinned.

"I used to live in Maine, remember," Jason said with a frown. "That was like camping every day." He looked at his Dad's face, the real excitement he saw there, and sighed. "But... I could get into camping." He narrowed his eyes. "There better be s'mores, though."

"Promise," Doug said with a smile.

● ● ● ● ● ● ● ● ● ● ● ● ●

After the house meeting, Marty and Taye went back to planning their trip, and Arthur went downstairs to pack. Ken lingered to take a cup of coffee in the kitchen, while Jason hit his homework in the living room. "So, whatcha think about Arthur moving, really?" Ken asked.

"I think it sucks," Doug admitted. "But I think it means that things are working out well with him and John, so I want to support him, of course."

Ken nodded. "Yeah, that's a big step. Movin' in." He added some sugar to the hot coffee, stirring it, slowly. "What do you think you'll do with Arthur's old place? Rent it out?"

"I dunno," Doug mused. "I hadn't gotten that far in thinking. We don't *need* the rent, and we've gotten lucky with who's moved in here overall." He smiled at his friend. "Present company included."

"Thanks," Ken said, grinning, clinking his coffee cup on Doug's and taking a sip. "Well... what would you think of lettin' me move down there? Like, throw you more rent, extra to cover utilities."

Doug blinked in surprise. "Uh... maybe? Don't you think you'd be kind of lost in there? I mean, Arthur made half the place into an art studio. You thinking of putting in a home gym, or something?"

"No," Ken said, thoughtfully. "I wanted to talk to everyone 'bout this, but I wanted to talk to you first." He sipped his coffee again. "I... if you're cool with it... if everyone is, I mean... I'd like to ask Michael... to move in with me." He quickly added, "That's why I'd wanna throw more rent an' utilities at you, assumin' you're okay with it at all."

Doug stared at the skinny man sitting in front of him. Move in? He *had* grown up a lot. "Wow, Ken... but, like you say, that's a big step. Are you sure?"

"Nope," Ken said, with a grin. "But I'm willin' to take a chance on this. Paulie once said Michael was good fer me, but he was only half-right. Actually, we're really good for each other." He rubbed the back of his neck. "I never had anyone I ever even thought of wanting to move in with, but with Michael... I feel closer to him than anyone since… well… in a long time." He sighed, then looked at Doug. "What do you think? If you don't think it's a good idea, I won't even bring it up. I haven't asked Michael yet."

"I think… that it's a fantastic idea," Doug said happily. "Ken, we're all crazy about Michael. Heck, at one point I thought we should've traded you for him," he said with a mischievous grin.

"Gee, thanks," Ken said, smirking.

"I know, I know. Well, it was before you… grew up." Doug smiled. "I'll ask the others, but, honestly, I can't imagine anyone having an issue with it."

"Awesome," Ken said. "Well, let me know what everyone says. Shit, I can't believe how nervous I am." He grinned, sheepishly. "I feel like a kid going on his first date. I dunno if Michael's the one, but, well, I wanna find out. An' I feel like we been t'gether long enough that movin' in is th' next step in findin' out."

"I think it's awesome, Ken," Doug said with a sincere smile. "I guess the question is more likely to be what to do with your old apartment then, isn't it? Well, like I say, we don't need the rent."

"If you're not gonna rent it," Jason's voice came, drifting from the living room, "I *so* call dibs."

"So you heard all that, huh squirt?" Doug chuckled.

"Yup." A few moments later, he spoke again, to say, "Good for you, Ken!"

• • • • • • • • • • • • •

The next few weeks passed in a flurry of activity. Marty's family came to visit, to see Taye and Marty before their trip to Europe, all except for his grandmother, Francine, who wasn't well. She was living in a retirement home now and seemed to take delight in tormenting all of the orderlies around her. Arthur packed up his belongings and moved out. He left most of the furniture behind for Ken and Michael. Michael seemed to be constantly smiling and blushing, like he couldn't believe what was happening. The two of them seemed as happy and content as Doug had ever seen a couple.

Two days later, Doug dropped Marty and Taye off at the airport in the evening for their trip. They had left him a long string of hotel contact information, and they had promised to send everyone postcards from every fabulous city they stayed in, and to bring back a ton of photos and souvenirs.

When he got home, Doug hugged Jason. "Place seems so quiet, all of a sudden."

"It won't when Ken gets home from his photo shoot," Jason snickered. "Those two can get loud."

Doug laughed. "You're not supposed to be listening in on *that*."

Jason made a face. "Eh. Like I want to. Like I said, they're *loud*."

That only made Doug laugh harder. "Well, til then, it's just us, buddy. Whatcha wanna do?"

"Um, well..." Jason ducked his head a little. "I kinda promised to go over Becky's for a study date. We got our finals comin' up."

"Oh," Doug said, blinking. "I knew that. It's marked on the calendar." He walked over and tapped the entry written in on their big wall chart. "Sorry, bud." He grinned. "You like Becky, huh?"

Jason flushed a little. "I think she's awesome," he said, honestly. "She's so... gorgeous, an' funny, an'... I'm just afraid... she might not like me as much as I like her."

Doug looked at his son. He was athletic, smart, generous, kind.... He felt like he could keep listing good qualities all day, but would struggle to find the truly bad ones. "I think she likes you just fine," he said with a smile. "Just... you know... if she *really* likes you..."

"Daaad," Jason said, looking mortified, "do *not* try to have the talk with me. Please."

"Well," Doug said with a grin, "when a mommy cat and a daddy cat love each other very much..."

Jason threw a couch pillow at his father. "Not listening! So not listening!"

"They begin to have certain urges..."

Jason laughed. "Stoppit! I'll wrap the banana, I swear!"

Doug laughed along with his son, then crossed the room, hugging him hard. "Go have a good time with Becky. Just not a *great* time, okay?"

"Okay, okay," Jason said, rolling his eyes, but he hugged back. "Love you, Dad."

"Love you, too, buddy," Doug said, closing his eyes.

Later, when he was alone, Doug sat, reading Paulie's journals a little. There wasn't much left to them, and the reading was becoming harder going. He found himself wishing Paulie had started keeping them earlier, that their whole life together had been chronicled like this. He flipped the pages until he came to the last, short entry, and frowned, softly. Then he flipped to the next page – a blank page. There was nothing more to read. Paulie had told him there were some pages left in one journal, and he'd already sorted aside the ones that were blank.

"Knock, knock," came a voice. "Someone is home, yes?"

"Hey there, Mrs. N." Doug stood up, coming to the top of the stairs. "Jason let you in?"

"Yes, he did. Such a good boy, Mr. Douglas Pope," Mrs. Nussbaum said with a smile, eyes shining behind her horn-rimmed glasses. "Very proud you should be of your part in his upbringing."

"And very proud I am indeed, Mrs. N.," Doug said, smiling, nodding. "To what do I owe this honor?"

"I am returning some of Paulie's books that you've leant me," she said, putting them down on the counter. "Also, I have made some chocolate rugelach, and I wanted to share."

"Oh, man, I love this stuff," Doug said, accepting the container. "You didn't tell Jason you'd brought it, did you?" He opened the container, popped a piece of the pastry into his mouth, and grinned around it.

"Yes, I did," she said, wagging a finger. "So don't be too greedy and eat it all before he gets home from his study date." She smiles. "A study date with a very nice girl I'm thinking, from what I've seen of her so far."

Doug grinned as he munched on the rugelach. "Becky's great, and Jason's crazy about her."

"Also, she is pretty crazy about him, or I'm going blind, maybe," she said, eyes crinkling up. "And how is Mr. Douglas Pope, hmm?"

"I'm good," Doug said with a firm nod. "I really am. I mean… it still hurts. I cry sometimes, when I think about him." He smiled a little bit. "But… I know he wouldn't want me to grieve forever. I can't believe it's been four months already. Is that too long a time to still feel like this? Too short?"

"Who knows?" Mrs. Nussbaum said, taking a piece of rugelach for herself and sitting on Paulie's writing chair. "I don't think there's exactly a hard and fast rule about these sorts of things. You'll grieve until you're done grieving. This is normal and human, yes?"

"I expect so, Mrs. N." He nodded behind her at the desk. "I was just reading Paulie's journals some more. I got to the end."

"Oh yes?" She looked at the journals and then nodded. "I think you're very lucky to have these treasures. When I lost my Herman, God rest his soul, I mourned, of course. Our Paulie helped me through that. Afterwards, however, I found I couldn't remember little things. Dates of when things had happened, the name of a restaurant we went to in Buffalo, what I'd worn the night we had our first date. If I had something like your journals..."

"Oh, I know exactly what you mean," Doug said, nodding. "I got to thinking about our time together a month or so ago, and I found there were so many things I couldn't quite bring to mind. It was like our time together was painted in broad strokes, but the little details had been smudged out." He touched the cover of the journal. "But I have these... everything about our last three years or so."

"Like I said," Mrs. Nussbaum said, smiling, "a treasure." She lifted her glasses and rubbed her eyes a little. "I'm happy you have them." She stood up. "Well, I'm not meaning to disturb. I came to deliver rugelach and rugelach is delivered." She smiled. "I'm thinking, perhaps, we should set a day and have some dinner?"

"I would love that Mrs. N.," Doug said with a warm smile. He looked at the journals and said, "I kind of want to try my hand at this myself. Keeping a journal. But I really don't know how to begin."

"You'll work it out," she said, patting his hand on the journal. "You're a very smart man." She leaned in and kissed his cheek. "Take care of yourself, Douglas."

After she was gone, Doug sat there for a time. He pulled out the loose pages of the first journal, smoothed them out again, and pondered. Paulie'd had a hard time getting started too, but he'd found a solution. Doug smiled with what felt like inspiration. He picked up a pen and began to write.

Dear Paulie,

He stopped. That didn't feel right. Maybe it would've, once, but now, keeping a journal like that would've felt more like living in the past, dwelling on what had already been. What he wanted to do was what Paulie had done, to set things down so that someone could read the journals afterwards and look back on the times, good and bad, that had been. He crossed out what he had written...

And then the smile grew on his face. He knew how to begin.

Dear Jason,

So, I've decided to pick up where Paulie left off. I want to keep this journal, not just for you, but for all of our family. I'm writing them to you, because you're my son, and my "heir" if you will, but I hope you'll share these stories and recollections with anyone you want to. Maybe someday, you'll share them with your kids to help them know what it was like growing up with their grandpa, and so they know who Paulie was.

As I write this, Arthur and John are now living over Triangle Books. Ken and Michael are going to move in together in the basement, but they're taking the whole moving process slow, just moving things a box at a time. Marty and Taye left together on their big adventure in Europe, but they'll be back in a month or so.

I just realized, when Marty moved in, there were six of us living at 6 Kinsey Circle. Now, there will be again. The more things change, the more they stay the same, huh?

As I write this, you're out on a date with Becky Barbarino. I see in the two of you the same kind of high school sweethearts I thought your Mom and I were. But I was in denial of who I was all through that period. I'm so glad you're growing up in a different world from the one I did, when being gay carried so much shame. I mean, the world's not ideal, but it's improving. If you are gay (and believe me, I don't think you are), then things will be very different for you than they were for me. In just a month, the first legal gay marriages are going to begin in Massachusetts. That's something I never thought I'd see happen in my lifetime. I'm sorry Paulie didn't get to see it during his.

I want to tell you a little something about Paulie. I know that you know that I loved him. That I still love him. What I'm not sure I ever explained to you in any adequate terms is that Paulie was absolutely my soulmate. I feel like we completed each other in a lot of important ways. I don't rule out the possibility of finding someone special later in my life, but there will never be another Paulie.

I hope that you'll have someone like that in your life, whether it's Becky Barbarino or someone totally different you haven't met yet. I really do want nothing but the best for you, my son. You've grown up into such a smart, caring, loving young man, and I'm so proud of you. I know Paulie was proud, and I know your mother would be, too.

In one of his first journal entries, Paulie said that there are no real beginnings or endings, which is sort of like a lyric from a Harry Chapin song. He's absolutely right. I thought that when Paulie died, it would be the end, in a way, but it wasn't. Paulie isn't with us anymore, but we'll never forget him, or all the incredible things he did for us, and all the wonderful things he taught us.

The most amazing things I learned from Paulie were just things about the way he lived his life. He took forever to get angry, and he forgave easily. He cared so much about everyone around him, even people he barely knew. He gave freely of his time, his wisdom (some of it extremely hard-won), his money, and his love. I'm so happy you two became friends, and that you came to think of him as a second Dad. I know he thought of you as the son he never had.

Arthur tried to tell me the same thing Paulie did, really. He said that his moving out wasn't an ending, but a beginning. He and John are beginning a new life together, one that they've kept on hold for a long time. I realize that now.

I think, of all of us, Arthur understood Paulie better than anyone. I could be wrong, but I think he's the one that introduced Paulie to Harry Chapin. Do you know Harry Chapin? One of his songs is one of the things that made me want to be a better father to you. I'll have to play you some of his music some time.

I'll try to keep these journal entries up to date, when I can. If nothing major is going on, maybe I'll write down some stories about Paulie, me, and the others from before you came to live with us. I'd like you to know him better.

I'll sign off for now. I can't wait to see you when you get home.

Love, Dad

Thanks and Afterword

So, here we are, coming to an end, finally. Hard to believe, but it's been over thirteen years since we started this crazy journey. A lot of people have made Circles possible, and they all deserve thanks. I'll try my best to remember everyone.

Obviously, a huge thanks goes to Steve "iyu" Domanski and Scott "K-9" Fabianek. Although other people sat in with us and made story suggestions at times, the three of us were responsible for creating the core six characters and most of the ancillary characters of the series. We also plotted out the story more or less from beginning to end before a single word of it was down on paper.

Sean and Andy Rabbitt, who were also in on a lot of those preliminary story discussions, deserve huge thanks. Without them, this comic very likely never would have existed.

Jay "Teko" Nungesser did a lot of the typesetting work on the last couple of issues of the comic that were released, which was awesome, because I hated doing it. He has also been an invaluable resource as a fan that I could bounce some thoughts off of, as well as being a heck of a good friend. Thanks, Ottah.

Mike "Bazil" Eichner gets credit for suggesting, many moons back, that it might be interesting if one of the characters had been married and/or had a kid. That idea actually gelled before Issue 2, and the original dialogue for that issue had Doug mentioning he'd been married. It also resulted in Jason, a character I really enjoyed writing. He kind of blossomed into a more major character as I worked on the novel, because he had grown into someone I wanted to know more about.

A lot of things have happened since we started Circles. On the National front, gay marriage isn't just something being recognized at the state level any more, as gay couples are just now starting to gain federal recognition. When gay marriage became legal in Massachusetts, I looked at our timeline and thought, "Well, shit. Paulie and Doug missed out by just a few months." It really underlines for me how lucky I am that Steve and I, and Scott and his fella Ben, have been to live in an era of unparalleled acceptance for gay people in this country. A friend of mine from high school now has a 13-year old son of her own who is gay and coming out. When I was 13, I couldn't have imagined coming out. I'm glad he lives in this brave new world.

On a more personal level, over the last five years, I've lost both of my parents, as well as my last surviving grandparent. I've known since the beginning that Paulie would not survive the series (although we held out hope for a cure), but I hadn't lost many people I was very close to when we started the story. In a way, writing the ending of Circles now was more poignant and relevant for me than I think it would've been if I'd written it back in 2004. I understand loss and grief far better now than I did then, and I suspect that I wrote the whole scene with more real emotion than I would've if I'd written it before those personal losses.

It's worth mentioning that, while the story always evolved based on the times, the story itself evolved. Originally, for example, there had been the idea that Marty, John, and Arthur would actually have a threesome in issue 11. As I tried to write it, however, I couldn't believe in it. Arthur was too good a guy, John wasn't the pushy bastard we'd originally imagined him as, and Marty, although capable, as Paulie once did, of making a drunken mistake, was too loyal to Taye to betray him once his name was mentioned. I realized that, knowing Marty and Arthur as I did now, a kiss would be enough to cause them both huge guilt, and it would be enough to propel the story through.

Music has always played a huge part in Circles, from singing waiters at a fictional restaurant (although there are some similar restaurants now — I demand royalties for my idea!) to characters performing on stage. Every chapter title was a song lyric, and I wanted to give a comprehensive list of the songs they came from.

"All My Life's a Circle" – *Circle*, by Harry Chapin. This song was a huge influence on the whole theme of the series, really, including inspiring the title.

"Listen. Do You Want to Know a Secret?" – *Do You Want to Know a Secret*, by The Beatles.

"With the Moon Keeping Watch Over Me" – *On My Way*, by Phil Collins, from the Brother Bear soundtrack. This chapter is a short story originally written for the conbook for Feral! 2004 when Steve and I were guests of honor. It appears in the collected version of issues 1-4.

Part 1. "Paper Faces on Parade" – *Masquerade*, from the Phantom of the Opera soundtrack.

Part 2. "Steppin' Out" – *Steppin' Out*, by Joe Jackson.

"In His Anger and His Shame" – *The Boxer*, Simon & Garfunkel.

"A Time of Innocence" – *Bookends*, Simon & Garfunkel. I'm not sure how I let 2 back to back S&G songs get into the mix, but the titles both really worked for me.

"Life Is What Happens to You While You're Busy Making Other Plans" – *Beautiful Boy*, by John Lennon.

"Isn't Anyone Trying to Find Me?" – *I'm With You*, by Avril Lavigne. I'm not her biggest fan, but this song is kind of haunting, and it fit the right mood for Arthur and John's emotions following Paulie getting infected.

"I Was Meant for the Stage" – *I Was Meant for the Stage*, by the Decemberists.

"Take Your Mind Back, I Don't Know When" – *Real Men*, by Joe Jackson. This song blew me away when I was a teenager. No one came out then, but here was Joe Jackson thumbing his nose at the world. I have nothing but admiration for the sheer level of sack he showed, and I love this song so much.

Part 1: "In Your Wildest Dreams" – *Your Wildest Dreams*, by the Moody Blues.

Part 2: "Why Can't I Sing It, Too?" – *New Music*, from Ragtime.

Part 3: "There's a Lot of Us Running Around" – *Goofy Boy*, by Farrenheit, a band my brother was in. They were awesome, and still are when they get together now and then.

Part 4: "Walking This High Road" – *The Mighty*, by Sting, from the soundtrack of The Mighty.

"We Have to Pay for the Love We Stole" – *The Dark End of the Street*, by lots of people, but my favorite is by The Commitments.

"Measure It in Love" – *Seasons of Love*, from the soundtrack of Rent. This play was an enormous influence on the whole story of Circles, in a way. If not for this brilliant piece of work, I wouldn't have wanted to tell the story of someone who was HIV+, as my own personal experiences with losing people I knew and cared about to this pandemic were very sad ones.

"Sunrise and Sundown" – *Circle*, by Harry Chapin.

I want to end this on what could be construed as a kind of a cornball note, but which is completely true, nonetheless. The only reason you're holding this book now is because of the support of the people who loved the original issues of the comic. Over the years, we've met plenty of them at cons, and I know they've been waiting patiently (and sometimes not so patiently) to find out how the story ended.

To those fans, I want to really reach out and thank you. If you hadn't shown so plainly how much you cared about this project, then when Scott made it clear he wouldn't have time to finish *Circles* as a comic, I might've just done a quick post online to say how it was meant to have ended and then moved on to other projects. But that didn't seem worthy, somehow, of all the kind words we've had from fans over the years.

I still get e-mails from people who want to let us know how much *Circles* touched them. I've heard stories about people who were inspired to come out because of it, or who read it at a point in their lives when they needed some inspiration, and found it through the trials and joys of our fictional creations.

While I have no other stories planned with the characters from *Circles*, the boys from 6 Kinsey Circle will always hold a special place in my heart. It has been my honor to bring closure to them, to our fans, and to myself and the other creators. There will be other comics, books, and stories, I have no doubt, but this one was something special.

With love, from Boston.

- Andy

Learn more about **Rabbit Valley® Books and Comics** at
www.rabbitvalley.com

Made in the USA
Columbia, SC
27 September 2021